SILENT SECRETS

SILENT SECRETS

Cindy LaChance

authorHOUSE®

AuthorHouse™
1663 Liberty Drive
Bloomington, IN 47403
www.authorhouse.com
Phone: 1-800-839-8640

© 2013 by Cindy LaChance. All rights reserved.

No part of this book may be reproduced, stored in a retrieval system, or transmitted by any means without the written permission of the author.

Published by AuthorHouse   06/28/2013

ISBN: 978-1-4817-7202-0 (sc)
ISBN: 978-1-4817-7203-7 (e)

Library of Congress Control Number: 2013911702

Any people depicted in stock imagery provided by Thinkstock are models, and such images are being used for illustrative purposes only.
Certain stock imagery © Thinkstock.

This book is printed on acid-free paper.

Because of the dynamic nature of the Internet, any web addresses or links contained in this book may have changed since publication and may no longer be valid. The views expressed in this work are solely those of the author and do not necessarily reflect the views of the publisher, and the publisher hereby disclaims any responsibility for them.

Prologue

Night enveloped the cabin, bringing darkness into the small room where the girls sat alone on the floor. The two were amusing themselves with their collection of small shells and rocks, making various designs on the bare wood floor. All the while, neither was making a sound. This was usually how they spent their time when they were alone in the cabin.

Both silently hoped their father would return tonight, and yet at the same time did not want him to. The food supply was limited and both were hoping he would remember to bring something for them to eat home with him this time. It didn't always happen.

Since he had not returned last night, they were sure tonight he would be home. With what and in what condition was the question.

With that thought, Edith quickly glanced around the small cabin. The dishes were washed and put away and the wood floor of the kitchen/sitting room had been swept clean. Nothing was out of place, not that there was much in the small two room cabin that could be out of place. She knew it was important to make sure the place was clean enough for him when he did arrive, that way it was less likely he would explode.

June started quietly singing a little song that their mother had taught her before she had died the previous year. Edith smiled at her younger sister's lilting voice, but did not join in; she never did.

Both girls looked up from their game at the sound of feet banging on the wooden step outside. Their father was home. Edith jumped up to open the door after he yelled out for her to do so. At the same time, June quickly gathered the shells and stored them in the small box the girls kept hidden under their bed. Their father would never approve of their game and neither wanted the shells to be broken as he would likely do.

From the sound of his voice, they knew he had been drinking, as he did often since their mother's death. He entered the cabin, carrying two brown paper bags of groceries, which he slammed onto the scarred table in the center of the room. The sound exploded in the small quiet room.

"What the hell is wrong with you, can't you even open the door when I come home with my hands full. You're as useless as always." He slurred, looking at Edith, while ignoring June, who had remained sitting on the floor, hiding the box behind her back.

"Get this stuff put away, and don't be all night doing it."

He lumbered past Edith, hitting her absently on the back of the head as he passed by. June stood slowly and quietly made her way to the single bedroom with the small box of shells clasped tightly to her chest. After sliding the box as far under the bed as she could, she hid under the few covers on the bed, away from the anger in the other room. She could still hear the loud voice of her father, berating her sister as he so often did.

Even with the door almost closed and the blankets over her head, June could hear Edith putting the contents of the bags on the few open shelves in the other room. All the while her father continued to complain, mostly mumbling to himself.

Finally Edith crawled quietly under the covers in the small bed, holding June close and shaking in silence at the same time. June held her tightly as well, aware of the tears sliding down Edith's face. June did not know what to say and was certainly not expecting her sister to say anything to her about what had just happened beyond the now closed door. This was not the first time the girls had gone to bed like this and neither expected it would be the last.

Blessed silence came from the other room now. Their father had obviously fallen asleep on the small cot, or maybe he had passed out in the only armchair in the room.

That is, if he had not left the girls alone again.

Chapter 1

The predominantly residential street was fairly quiet for a Saturday morning as Ron made his way along the sidewalk to his aunts' home. He felt the crispness of fall in the air around him and could see the changes nature was making happening as he walked. He glanced up to see the sunshine breaking through the leaves. The previous green leaves were now brilliant hues of red, orange and yellow. Each leaf blowing in the gentle wind, some twirling to the ground, only to be blown down the road or gather in piles against the house fronts and fences.

Ron liked the fall season well enough, with all the wonderful changes to the leaves, much like he felt in the spring when the flowers were reawakened by the hot sun and longer days. Removing a yellow leaf, which had landed on his head, Ron mused on what he didn't like about this particular season. Regretfully it meant winter would soon be here.

Winter in southern Ontario could be challenging, to say the least. He was envisioning the falling snow in his mind and for a second could almost feel the icy northern wind blowing. He thought of the havoc caused by the inevitable snowstorms, freezing rain and the occasional ice storms. Ron was glad during those times that he didn't own a car. Walking was hazardous enough, but in a car, with all the other idiots he saw on the winter roads . . . no way.

As he continued towards his destination he debated again for the hundredth time about moving to a warmer climate. He thought about this just about every fall with the internal debate always progressing the same way. He could apply for a job in some tropical country, enjoying the warm weather all year long. His days of snow and cold would be over, as easy as that.

He knew now, as he always knew, even as the pleasant thought went through his mind that he would never actually leave. Ontario was his home, unpredictable, ever changing, cold weather and all. The constantly changing weather had its appeal at times, except of course in late January and February when the wind chill could bring bone chilling temperatures which made him want to be any where else. Just the thought of this made him shiver. Regardless, the reality was that all his friends, his family and his job were all here, and so he would stay.

Besides, he smiled to himself; he did enjoy watching the kids playing in the snow, even though they weren't supposed to do this at school any more. The rules said no throwing snow, there could be a hidden rock or a piece of ice inside the snowball. Some one could get hurt, or worse some kid could get upset and their parents would sue the school board. There fore it was better to just prevent any thing at all from happening. Make the rules to ensure no one had any fun or interacted without the express permission of the school. That way no one would get hurt and never have the opportunity to learn from their mistakes. That was his take on the basic policy of the school boards, as far as Ron was concerned. Sometimes life had just to many rules for our own good, he thought.

Silent Secrets

Today Ron was once again on his way to see his aunt, his mother's sister. Ever since he could remember he had made the trip to visit her every Saturday. First as a young boy, this trip had been with his mother at his side. They would go for a visit, almost always on Saturday when his aunt did not have to work or when he did not have to go to school. At times he had resented these visits when he would rather be out playing with his friends, but of course he could never say that at the time. His mother would have been upset and disappointed in him.

As Ron had gotten older, he had wanted to stop this routine, however his mother, with her persuasive charm and the skill only a mother possesses, had made him promise to always visit his aunt at least once a week. She had said, "Your company cheers the old woman up, and keeps her connected to the outside world". She was a very determined woman when she wanted to be. So Ron had continued the weekly trek to his aunt's home every Saturday.

Ron knew full well that she didn't go out much since she had stopped working. She preferred instead to remain in her home, completely alone in her big two-storey house. Ron could, in some ways, understand this; sometimes having no one around was a good thing.

He had stopped visiting for a while when he was away at teachers college. But once he had returned from his studies, his mother had insisted that he continue the old established pattern of weekly visits. He could not disappoint her, especially since she asked very little of him for the most part. His mother also informed him that she could not easily get around now herself, suffering arthritis in her legs, especially in the cold or damp weather. If not for Ron, his aunt would have no one to visit her.

So the full responsibility of visiting the old woman fell to him. Ron had promised his mother and himself, so here he was, spending another Saturday morning visiting with a woman who didn't talk to him no matter how long he stayed.

When it came right down to it, he didn't really mind the visits, especially now that he was an adult and could understand a little more. After all these years the visits had become part of his weekend routine, along with getting his weekly groceries, grading papers and doing the laundry down at the corner Laundromat. Even during the rare times he had a girlfriend, he managed to visit regularly.

He transferred the bag of groceries to his other arm, being careful not to squash the bread. That would certainly annoy his aunt. That was one trait the two sisters shared, they both had the ability to let you know when they were upset without ever uttering a word.

He could picture her face now in his mind. She would take the bread from the top of the bag; look at the dented section as she ran her old fingers over the plastic, shaking her head while frowning at the loaf of bread in her hand. But of course she would not say anything to him, never verbally reprimand him for this indiscretion, but he would know her displeasure nonetheless. It was best to just be careful and avoid her disappointment altogether.

He always made a point to pick up a few basic items for her each week when he did his own shopping. He had decided long ago, once he was old enough to be less selfish of his time, that it was not that big an imposition; just visit once a week, bring her a few basics and stay for an hour or so. That way he made both his aunt and his mother feel better with one simple activity. Not really that much to ask of a person.

Today as he approached her weatherworn house nestled between several other better-maintained homes, he noticed Mr. Wells on the sidewalk outside his own door. He was busy sweeping the crisp multi coloured leaves from the steps of his house. The job seemed a pointless task to Ron, but what the heck, what else does a lonely old man of 86 have to do with his time? It was still nice enough weather to be outside, at least until the snow and cold came. Ron imagined the winters' wind and snow would keep the older citizens cooped up for months on end, while he himself had to slug through the snow and slush to get to work, as Mr. Wells likely had to do in his day. Such is the cycle of life, he mused.

"Good day, Mr. Wells." Ron called out loudly as he approached, not wanting to startle the old man.

Mr. Wells would never admit that his hearing was not what it used to be, and refused to wear the hearing aid Ron knew his doctor had given him. Knowing this, Ron always made sure to speak loudly when ever they met. This had been his practice for years and he didn't even think about it any longer. Mr. Wells slowly turned at the sound of Ron's voice, his face brightening in recognition.

"Little Ronny, how nice to see you. Here to see Edith, are you? Such a nice day for a stroll, wouldn't you say? The wind has picked up a bit, don't you think? Sure hope we don't get rain. Will you be staying long? Why don't you drop over to see us before you leave?" He leaned heavily on his broom for support while he spoke.

Mr. Wells had always had the habit of asking a string of questions before anyone could have a chance to answer any one of them. Ron just smiled and agreed that it was indeed a nice day for a stroll and a visit with Edith.

Just then the wind picked up even more, blowing even more leaves on to the steps that Mr. Wells had just been sweeping.

"Damn wind," said Mr. Wells, still leaning on the handle of his broom while shaking his head slowly from side to side.

"Every year it's the same thing. I sweep the leaves off the steps and the wind blows them right back on. I wouldn't bother with all this myself, you know, except that Mrs. Wells always insists they stay clean. 'What would the neighbors think if we just let the house fall down around our heads?' he quoted his wife in a high-pitched voice, which sounded very much like her. He rolled his eyes as he said this.

"My mom is the same way. I remember her always being after my dad to keep the grass cut and the garden weeded. Maybe that's why I live in an apartment."

Silent Secrets

"Women," Mr. Wells said to Ron as he winked and glanced quickly at his front window. Ron glanced in that direction as well. Neither man saw anyone at the window. For this, Ron was glad.

"She musta gone off to make you some cookies, Ronnie, instead of watching me do all this work. They're always asking the impossible from us men folk. Ain't that right? Oh well, we love 'em anyways." Mr. Wells smiled.

Ron smiled at the old man. "And how is your wife today, Mr. Wells?" he shouted, to ensure he was heard above the increasing wind and the resistance of the old man to his hearing aid.

Ron knew that besides not admitting that his hearing was not what it used to be, Mr. Wells would also not admit that Mrs. Wells was not what she used to be. In fact, Mrs. Wells had passed away over two years ago, but Mr. Wells continued to live in his own world, which in his mind included the woman he had loved for over fifty years. He still talked as if she were sitting in the house, watching them now from the big front window in the living room.

Ron had decided this was harmless enough in and of itself, but still, he thought, it was kind of eerie. He imagined Mr. Wells having conversations over breakfast with the empty chair across the table, deciding what chores needed to be completed each day based on the whims and desires of a dead woman. He wondered if he would be the same if he were ever married to someone as long as Mr. and Mrs. Wells had been married.

Ron used to try to remind Mr. Wells that his wife was no longer with them. It was something he thought he should do to help the poor man adjust to the situation, but now he had given up worrying about it. Mr. Wells had just ignored any comments as if they had not been said anyway, so Ron figured, what the heck, he's not hurting any one. Now Ron always made a point of asking after Mrs. Wells if the old man brought her up. What Ron could not do was get out of the habit of calling this old friend anything but Mr. Wells.

Ron had spent a lot of time with the couple during his years of visiting this neighbourhood. They knew him well and he knew them. He also knew the couple had never had children of their own, so had always treated 'Little Ronnie' like part of their own family.

"Oh well, you know, she's fine, just fine. Keeping her self busy as usual. You know what she's like, always puttering away at something. I imagine she'll be going to get her hair all done up again soon. I'll let her know you were asking though, she'll be pleased with that. I haven't seen Edith today but I took her a couple of those little notebooks earlier in the week. Found them on sale down at the drug store when I was there. I know how much she likes to write stuff down." Mr. Wells rambled on.

"Well, that was very nice of you, Mr. Wells. I had meant to bring some myself and forgot."

Oh, it's no trouble at all. I walk down there every day anyway. Just for the exercise you understand, but if I see something, I don't mind picking it up. Have you been keeping yourself busy and out of trouble, Ronnie? Mr Wells asked with a wink.

"I've been pretty busy this week, lots of new routines to get used to at school. Every year it seems the rules change and I have to start all over again. Just getting the names straight each year can be challenging enough for me sometimes." Ron joked.

"Yeah, I know what you mean, sometimes I can't remember names either, that's why I always call my wife dear. It wouldn't do to call out the wrong name, no siree!" Mr. Wells glanced again at the window and appeared relieved that it remained empty.

"I'm sure aunt Edith appreciated the books. I guess I'll pop in to see her now. I'll talk to you again, Mr. Wells. Good luck with the leaves."

Ron waved to Mr. Wells as he passed on to the next house, going carefully up the steps to his aunts' door. Here the leaves still remained and had formed a small colourful pile at the base of each step. With any luck, the wind would carry them away. Maybe next weekend when the trees had completed their shedding for yet another year he would help clean these up, at least that would be something they could do during his visit. Ron was pretty sure there would be plenty of leaves still lying around next weekend. Today after his visit he already had plans, other wise they could do it today.

He thought briefly about his aunt's notebooks, wondering what, besides answers to people's questions, she actually wrote in all those little books every one brought her. He hadn't actually ever looked at any of her books except the one page she might be using when he visited. All these years and he really knew very little about her. Strange how you realize things all at once about the people you think you know, he thought.

Chapter 2

Ron knocked loudly on the old green, weather beaten door, waiting patiently on the step in the cool wind. He was still hoping against hope that the cold winter weather would hold off for a bit. Perhaps the fabled "Indian Summer" would last longer than usual, keeping the nice sun filled days and not to cool evenings available for him to enjoy. Not being a winter sports buff certainly had its disadvantages for those living in Canada. He knew, however, that the seasons' clock was ticking quickly against that faint hope, regardless of how much he wanted to think otherwise.

As he waited for the door to open, he thought of his own apartment, which was always so drafty when the cold north winter wind blew. The old windows and poorly insulated walls did not offer much protection from the mighty gusts that so often ravaged the city throughout the winter, but it was all he could afford. Actually, it was more like it was all he wanted to afford.

He preferred instead to save his money for other things, not just some place to sleep and occasionally eat. Any thing else would just be a waste of his hard earned money.

He waited, musing on possible winter vacation spots he could look into for this year's winter break. His aunt did not answer his knock immediately as she usually did. Ron knocked again, louder this time, calling out her name loud enough that even Mr. Wells could hear him.

He had not of course called ahead to let her know what time he would be arriving; that would be impossible. His aunt had never had a phone installed in her home as far as he knew. She certainly hadn't had one that he could ever remember. Since she could not talk, she had explained, in her writing, she had never seen the need for one.

Still she didn't answer the door, so he gently turned the knob to open the door and called out to her again.

"Aunt Edith, it's Ron, are you home?" His voice echoed down the dark hall.

Edith might not be able to talk, but unlike Mr. Wells, there was nothing wrong with her hearing. If she were home, he knew, she would come to the door right away at the sound of her only nephew's voice. No one came. Edith was not one to go out at the best of times these days, preferring instead to stay in her home and have what she needed brought to her with the help of her neighbours or himself.

Even if she did go somewhere, she would never go out and leave her door unlocked. She did not trust any one that much. With the door unlocked, she must be here, Ron thought apprehensively. Perhaps she was in the garden out back, completing some last minute task in her beloved garden.

He stepped into the dark cluttered hallway and closed the door, shutting out the wind as well as the small amount of light offered by the opening. The hall way was immediately dark and Ron waited while his eyes adjusted to the dim surroundings after being in the bright fall sunshine. He glanced quickly into the living room to the right of the hall but did not see his aunt in the dark and cluttered room.

Ron walked the length of the hall, which led directly to the kitchen, calling out to her again as he approached the room. He didn't want to scare her. He was hoping she was there, to engrossed in one of her many books to hear him or working in the back yard, as he had originally thought. He glanced briefly at the stairs as he passed; he had never been upstairs in the old house and did not fancy going up today. As it was he had to step carefully around piles of papers and boxes she had stored in the hall.

His aunt was a pack rat, and even that was an understatement. There were piles of clutter taking up most of the space in the house. Judging by the amount of items she had in the living and dining rooms on this floor, he could just imagine what had been stored over the years in the unused rooms of the second floor. The only really clear space was the kitchen table and counters. That area she always kept clean.

As Ron reached the kitchen doorway, he saw his aunt on the floor, lying on her back, not moving. He could see her eyes were closed.

Fear gripped him immediately as he rushed to her, dropping the bag as he reached her. As he knelt beside her on the worn linoleum floor beside the table, he saw also that a kitchen chair had been over turned.

"Aunt Edith, are you alright? Aunt Edith!" Ron yelled.

She did not respond to his calls. Her eyes remained closed. Ron could see she was breathing, shallow as it was, her chest moving just slightly, but he could not rouse her. She did not respond to his concerned call.

He left her where she lay, rushed out the front door and toward Mr. Wells. He was still sweeping the same leaves into the same pointless piles.

"Mr. Wells, I need to use your phone. Aunt Edith has collapsed. I think she needs an ambulance."

Without waiting for the old man to reply, he ran around him, and up the steps to his house, taking them two at a time. He ran directly into the living room, grabbing the cradled phone from the end table. With shaking fingers, he punched in 911.

When his call was answered, he blurted into the phone.

"I need an ambulance, my aunt has collapsed. What? Yes, she's still breathing."

"Okay, sir, an ambulance has been dispatched. Just remain on the line with me until they arrive." The calming voice did not relieve Ron's anxiety.

"I can't, I left her next door, I have to get back to her. She's in there all alone. Please hurry. I don't know what's wrong with her."

He quickly gave his aunt's address, and then hung up to race back to his aunt in the house next door.

When he reached the kitchen, Mr. Wells was standing by the table, gazing down at the prone woman on the floor. Strangely it occurred to Ron that he had not thought Mr. Wells could move that fast.

"Edith, Edith, are you alright?" Mr. Wells called out loudly before glancing at Ron in the doorway.

"Mr. Wells," Ron yelled, fear edging his voice, "can you go outside and show the ambulance attendants in? They're on their way."

As Mr. Wells shuffled from the kitchen to carry out Ron's request, Ron again knelt down beside his aunt, picking up her hand, gently calling her name. He didn't really know what to do, but this seemed like the right thing.

"Where are they?" Ron muttered to himself.

Time stood still in the small kitchen for Ron. Thankfully a few short minutes later he heard the ambulance attendants coming through the front door of his aunt's house.

"Excuse me sir, let me in there please," the first attendant stated as he put his hand on Ron's shoulder. "Please step back, sir."

"Can you tell me what happened?" the attendant asked as he leaned over Edith as Ron had stepped out of the way. He checked for her pulse and gently lifted her eye lids while shining a small light into her eyes.

"I don't know, I just came in the house and found her lying here like this," Ron sputtered.

"What's her name? Is she on any medication? Does she have any allergies?" the attendant asked rapidly as he worked over Edith. The string of questions reminded Ron of Mr. Wells.

"Her name is Edith McKellridge. I don't know about any medications or allergies. She's my aunt. Is she going to be all right?" Ron asked.

"You don't know if your aunt takes medication? The attendant asked, looking at Ron.

"No, I've never seen any medication, but I don't live here."

The second attendant had arrived in the kitchen with the gurney. The two attendants spoke to each other quickly in a lingo that meant little to Ron, rhyming off numbers for blood pressure and heart rate, talking about stats and status. None of this told Ron anything about what was wrong with his aunt or if she would be okay. Ron wanted desperately to know what they were talking about, but remained quiet as they worked.

One attendant continued to call her name as the other spoke quickly and quietly into a handset attached to his shoulder. All Ron could do was stand back while listening and watching the activity on the floor. Edith, despite the attempts made by the attendants, had not yet opened her eyes or responded in any way to the calls of her name.

"We're taking her over to Memorial, sir. Her pulse is very weak. Are you sure you don't know about any present medications?" the attendant asked again.

"No, no, I don't have any idea. I was just coming to visit today. Is she going to be all right? Can I go to the hospital with her?" Ron knew he was babbling.

"Well, you can meet us at the hospital if you want. We're going to take her in now. She needs a full medical assessment. The hospital is expecting her."

Together the two attendants picked up his aunt, placed her gently on the gurney, securely strapped her in and covered her with a light yellow blanket. All this Ron saw and registered and yet everything still seemed surreal, like watching a movie about other people, from the neutral position of his living room.

As the attendants started down the hall with his aunt, Ron called out to them, "Oh, I almost forgot. Edith is mute."

The attendants looked at him for a second, then continued on their way. Ron told them he would meet them at the hospital.

"I have to call my mom, let her know what's happened," Ron said to no one in particular, as the gurney and his aunt went down the hallway and out the front door. Ron watched as she was secured in the back of the ambulance. One attendant stepped into the back with her, the other closing the door behind them. The ambulance drove off with the lights and siren wailing into the still bright, crisp mid morning air. Ron thought, sirens were never a good sign.

Mr. Wells had remained on the sidewalk, now letting the leaves blow where they wanted, no longer concerned about what either his dead wife or the neighbours might say.

Ron turned to Mr. Wells, the concern they both felt evident on their grim faces and furrowed brows. The silent worry was passing like a bolt of lightning from one to the other.

"Mr. Wells, I need to use your phone again, okay?"

"Of course son, you help yourself. Do what ever you need to do. Don't you worry about Edith. I'm sure she'll be fine. She's a tough one, that aunt of yours. We've known her a lot of years. She's always been healthy as a horse, except for the voice thing of course."

Mr. Wells continued talking, but Ron did not hear. He was no longer listening, thinking only of contacting his mother and getting to the hospital to be with his aunt. She would be very upset when she woke up there.

Ron returned to Mr. Wells' home and the only close phone available. He needed to call his mother. While he waited for her to answer, he glanced around the living room in which he stood. Ron tapped his foot impatiently as the phone rang in his ear.

Little had changed in this room from when he had come over while visiting his aunt as a small boy, he noticed. He would regularly stop in so he could pick up the special baked treats Mrs. Wells always made for him: chocolate cookies sprinkled with coconut. He hadn't had any for many years and right now he wished he were here with his small hands outstretched to pick up a fresh batch.

Ron knew Mr. Wells had someone come in once a week to help keep the place clean, his aunt had told him so. Redecorating clearly was not in their job description. The room still looked like a flashback from the late sixties. It made him smile to realize this house, like his aunts', never really changed and probably would not until someone new moved in. The worn couch on which he had sat waiting for his treats remained in the same spot, the same throw pillows propped against the arms.

As he was thinking of this his mother finally answered the phone, bringing him back to the present.

"Thank god you're home. I was worried you might be at the church." Ron said quickly into the phone. She sometimes spent Saturday mornings at her church, performing various volunteer services.

"Ron, what's wrong?" his mother asked, worry creeping into her voice.

"Mom, Aunt Edith has collapsed." Ron sputtered into the mouth piece.

"What? Is she okay, Ron?" his mother asked quietly, remaining calm, as was her nature.

"I'm not sure mom. She was on the floor in the kitchen when I arrived today. I called an ambulance but I don't really understand what the attendants were saying. I'm going to head over there now. They've taken her to Memorial down town. Oh, I told you that already. Anyway, I can come get you."

"Why don't you just go and see how she is. I'm sure she's fine, maybe just a little over tired or something. I'm not really feeling up to a trip to the hospital, dear."

Ron knew, before he had even asked, that she would not be anxious to go to the hospital and wait there with him. The last time she had waited at the hospital had been for his father. That had turned out to be a horrible experience for every one involved, including himself, but most importantly, his father. Ron asked about any medications for Edith.

"I'm pretty certain Edith didn't take any medications. Any prescribed medications would mean she had been to a doctor and we both know that's not likely, given her resistance to what she always referred to as 'the quacks'." Ron had to agree with that logic. He at least knew that much about his aunt.

After hanging up with his mother, Ron called a cab. Memorial was nearly 12 blocks from Edith's house and he didn't want to take the time to walk. This was one of the few times he wished he did own a car.

He was worried about what might be happening with his aunt. More importantly, he was anxious to find out what had caused her to collapse. Anxiety caused his heart to beat faster wondering how Edith was managing at the hospital. The doctors would have their hands full with her, he thought. Voice or no voice, they would figure out quickly enough she did not want their assistance.

Mr. Wells shuffled in to his living room just as Ron hung up with the cab company.

"Thanks for your help, Mr. Wells. I'm going over to the hospital to see how she is making out. I'll let you know how she is as soon as I can"

"You go take care of things, Ronny. I'll keep an eye on the house while you're gone. Don't you worry, Edith will be just fine."

Ron left the house and raced back to his aunts'. He grabbed the house keys from the hook in the front hall, closing and locking the door just as the blue and white cab pulled up and honked the horn.

At the hospital, the over crowded waiting room was busy and loud. The voices of the people engaged in various conversations, all occurring at once, blared in his ears.

"Excuse me. I'm here to see my aunt. She just came in by ambulance. Her name is . . ." Ron attempted to inform the nurse at the window.

"Sir, please just sign in at the desk. You'll be called when someone is ready to see you." The nurse interrupted as he spoke. Her tone made it clear that he had no other alternative. Ron sat and waited as he had been instructed to do. Her curtness and manner gave Ron the impression that maybe she used to be a professional wrestler or possibly an army sergeant before joining the healing profession. She should be listened to, he decided, so he sat and waited in the busy, noisy waiting area.

He amused himself for a while with people watching, one of his most favourite, and at times, amusing activities. Some really interesting people were at the hospital on this particular Saturday morning. Interesting in a freaky kind of way, was what Ron really thought. That's what made watching people so fascinating for him.

As Ron sat watching, one young boy, maybe four or five years old, kept running up to him, staring at him, sticking out his tongue He would then turn and run back to the woman who must be his mother. The woman was reading an old magazine and had no idea, or perhaps no interest, in whatever the boy was up to. Ron was not sure what exactly he was doing either. However, the activity kept the boy busy and Ron amused, at least for the time being.

After he became bored with sticking out his tongue, the young boy changed activities to become a gymnast. Jumping from chair to chair and sometimes from the backs of the chairs to the floor, he moved with lightning speed, a whirlwind of constant motion. Still his mother remained engrossed in the magazine she held on her lap.

Ron thought that what ever might have been medically wrong with the boy when he arrived at the hospital had nothing to do with a loss of energy or any broken bones. However, with the way he was jumping around the waiting room, this could soon change. From her reaction so far, it was unlikely his mother was going to either prevent this inevitable injury or attend to the boy when it happened. Ron decided the boy was very lucky to be in a hospital waiting room.

He thought of when he had been a child. Active yes, without question, but had he been like this? He thought not. He would have been stilled by the simple look of either his mother or his father. No words would have been needed to tell him how to act in such a public place. He would have been expected to sit quietly and mind his manners. He thought briefly that this small boy could benefit from 'the look' before he ended up in some real trouble, like some of the kids Ron had in his classes.

Ron noticed another patient apparently waiting to be seen. This was a woman who looked to be about 25. Ron could see her arm was bleeding through the loosely covered red stained gauze, which she held in place with her other hand. Ron wondered why she was not being seen immediately? The woman sat quietly in her chair, not paying attention to the young gymnast or anyone else in the busy room. She was glancing often at the nurse's station. She caught Ron's eye once and smiled at him, but he felt uncomfortable with her gaze and quickly looked away.

He finally looked at her again after a few minutes and quietly watched as she took a pair of small sewing scissors from her pants pocket. He saw her scratch a line in her arm just above the bandage with the point of the scissors. The fresh scratched area darkened and began to weep thick red blood, which trickled down her arm and onto the bandage already there. As much as he didn't want to, Ron continued to watch, mesmerized by this strange self-mutilating behaviour. He now noticed that both of her arms were scarred with long lines. Those he could see appeared to have healed, leaving behind a faint white scar.

As she finished creating this new wound, still concentrating on her work, one of the nurses from the desk approached her, holding out her hand for the scissors. Neither initially said anything. The woman slowly passed over the shiny scissors, looking at her arm and smiling back at the nurse as she did so.

"You know you can't do that here, Amy. Now sit still and wait for the Doctor to see you. Do you have anything else on you? Do we need to search you again today?" The nurse continued to hold her hand out, possibly waiting for something else to be passed over.

The woman shook her head slowly from side to side, smiling slightly, while continuing to look at the droplets of blood forming on her arm. The nurse took the scissors, leaving the woman to eventually adjust the bandage herself in order to cover the new cut. Clearly the nurses were not as concerned about the blood as Ron had been. He was finally able to look away.

People, Ron thought as he shook his head. I'll never figure them out, but they can be fascinating to watch. It made him think that he must come from a very normal family where children were taught manners in public and no one cut themselves on purpose.

As much as Ron enjoyed watching other people and trying to figure them out, he wondered what others saw when they looked at him. He knew he was fairly plain with his short brown hair and fit but un-muscled body. His students often kidded him about his lack of muscles when they were running the track. At least, Ron thought to himself, I don't stand out in a crowd like some of the people here.

He grabbed the closest magazine and began leafing through it without really looking, trying to fill the time while he waited. What was taking so long, Ron wondered as he became increasingly more anxious about his aunt. Why were the doctors taking so long to come talk to him? They should at least come out to reassure him that everything was going to be okay, he thought. Surely his aunt was fine and stable by now. Like Mr. Wells had said, she was tough.

Chapter 3

After mindlessly leafing through the magazines for another forty-five minutes or so, a different nurse, luckily not the one from the professional wrestling team, curtly instructed him to follow her. Ron had hoped for an update on his aunt, but clearly this was not going to be given to him by this equally efficient nurse. So far his hospital visit had not been very positive.

She led him from the noise of the main waiting room and into what looked like an office reception area. Ron saw two beige couches flanking the long walls with a coffee table in the center. The table was covered with what looked like information sheets with diagrams, medication information and a few possibly newer, but less used, general interest magazines.

"Wait here. Someone will be with you soon", the nurse com wrestler informed him in her clipped voice.

"Can you tell me how my aunt is doing?" Ron asked as she started to close the door.

"Some one will be with you soon, was all the information he received.

Cindy LaChance

Ron did as he was told not knowing what else to do in a situation like this. He resented that his mother was not here. The upside of the move, Ron thought, was that the room was definitely quieter and more comfortable than the waiting room had been.

Ron wondered why he had been moved to this room if no one was willing to tell him anything. Maybe, he thought, they finally realized he was not sick or waiting to be seen by a doctor for himself. As this thought entered his mind and calmed him, a second and more concerning one was right behind. What if they had brought him back here to tell him his aunt was dead? This thought caused all his previous anxiety to return in a rush.

He tried to make himself as comfortable as possible in the small room, but not knowing what was going on, he could not relax. He realized this could very well be another long wait. He attempted to relax into the couch, determined to try not to jump to any more conclusions about his aunt. As he waited, he absently picked up a magazine from the table, a two year old slightly battered edition of Canadian Gardening. A he thumbed through the pages, his thoughts returning inevitably to his aunt. She was such a lonely old lady, with no one but his mom and himself; and her garden, which she loved so much.

That garden behind her house could be featured in a magazine like this, he thought, with all the work she puts into it. Especially those roses, which even Ron, with his limited interest in flowers, knew were beautiful. If only she looked after herself as well, he mused, I wouldn't be sitting here right now. He returned the magazine to the table. Closing his eyes to stave off an impending headache, he sat back to wait. For what, he didn't know.

The door suddenly opened, causing Ron to jump. A man and a woman entered the room, quickly closing the door quietly behind them. The chatter of voices and the sounds of all the various equipment from the hospitals' emergency area flooded his head when the door opened then gone in an instant, bringing him back to attention.

Both people were dressed in suits but neither had a white coat over top. Neither held a hospital chart or wore a stethoscope around their neck. To Ron, they did not look like the doctors he had been expecting. He sat forward on the couch expectantly.

"Excuse me, sir. Can we speak to you for a minute, please?" The man asked as he approached Ron. "I'm Detective Hubert and this is my partner, Detective O'Leary." He gestured behind him toward the woman who had remained just inside the door.

Ron could immediately tell that Detective Hubert was a take-charge kind of person. That was the advantage of being a 'people watcher'. Ron felt he was very good at reading people when he met them for the first time. This man, with his straight stance and direct eye contact displayed an attitude of experience and authority. His voice, loud and clear, demanded authority. His partner, Detective O'Leary, stood back as the introductions were being made. Her only addition was to nod in Ron's direction.

The big man held out his right hand, extended in a friendly gesture to Ron, so he took it automatically as he stood. He hadn't had much to do with the police in his life, and was initially taken aback by their entrance, not yet comprehending why they wanted to speak to him.

"What's going on? Are you sure it's me you're wanting to talk to? I'm just waiting to see a doctor, not the police," Ron stated, as he smiled at both detectives.

"Please, sit down, Mr . . . . ?"

"Oh, Ron. Ron Walker. Are you here about my aunt? Is she okay? They just brought her in by ambulance a while ago, well, quite a while ago actually. I'm just waiting here to see her." Ron stopped talking and returned to the couch, while the two detectives remained standing. This made him feel uncomfortable, although he could not say why.

"I'm afraid your aunt is not okay, sir. That's why we're here. We've just been speaking to Dr Main, the attending emergency room doctor. Dr Main reports your aunt to be in very serious condition. Apparently they have stabilized her for now, but any thing more specific than that, you'll have to ask the doctor about. Right now, my partner and I would like you to answer a few questions for us, if you wouldn't mind."

Detective Hubert continued to hold Ron in his steady gaze. He was a big man, standing well over 6 feet. He filled out the well-made suit to capacity, but not, it appeared, with any excess weight. Even his short crew cut added to the appearance of strength. It looked to Ron like under that nice expensive suit he would have well toned muscles from working out regularly. Ron felt underdressed in his track pants and sweatshirt he had thrown on this morning.

Well, they do want to talk to me, Ron thought. He didn't think it would ever be a good idea to say no to a guy like that when he wanted answers. Not that he had any intention of not talking to them; he just couldn't right now understand what they wanted with him.

He noticed that the other cop, Detective O'Leary, had yet to say any thing to Ron. She just remained standing by the door, silently watching him. He wondered if blocking the door was intended to keep others out or to keep him inside.

Glancing over at her, Ron briefly wished she would step up to talk to him. He noticed her dark hair just touching her shoulders and the casual way she stood, confident but not menacing, at least not to Ron. She didn't look as frightening as this big guy did. Instead, she just stood like a silent guard at the door. Ron turned back to Detective Hubert.

"Well, officer, I really don't understand what I can do for you. Why are you here? What could you possibly want with me? Are you sure it's me you're here to speak to? If my aunt is that sick, I need to go see her."

Ron sat still as he asked these questions, glancing from one officer to the other. Suddenly the only possible reason the police might be here occurred to him, hitting him like a bulldozer out of no where.

"Has something happened to my mother? Is she alright?" Fear flooded his head and was evident in his voice. "I just spoke to he;, she's waiting for me to call. Has she been hurt? Is she here?" Ron jumped up from the couch as the questions hung in the air.

"No sir, I don't know anything about your mother. Please sit back down." Detective Hubert patiently waited for Ron to sit down before he continued.

Ron returned to his seat, but he could only sit at the very edge of the couch, not knowing what to expect next.

"Mr. Walker, you said you're here because of your aunt. Do you live with her?"

"What? Oh, sorry. No, I don't. I have my own place. I mean, I was just coming to visit her today when I found her lying on her kitchen floor."

"Does any one live with your aunt?" Detective Hubert asked quickly, almost before Ron had finished answering his first question.

"No, she lives by herself." His brow furrowed as he let the answer hang in the air. Why would any one care if someone lived with his aunt, he wondered.

"Why are you asking all these questions about my aunt?"

"Mr. Walker, when was the last time you saw your aunt before today?" Again the detective was quick with the questions.

"I saw her last Saturday, in the afternoon. I visit every Saturday, well, usually every Saturday. Are you trying to say she's been lying there for a week? No, wait. That's not possible. Mr. Wells said . . ." he was interrupted before he could finish.

"Did your aunt say anything to you this morning when you arrived? And by the way, what time was that?"

"I'm not sure what time exactly, sometime around ten, I think. My aunt didn't say anything. My aunt never speaks, detective. She's mute. So, no, she didn't say anything. I told that to the ambulance guys before they left.

"What exactly happened this morning?"

"When I arrived, she didn't answer the door, so I went in and found her lying on the kitchen floor. I called 911 as soon as I found her. I didn't know what was wrong with her or what else to do. Can't you please tell me what's going on?" Wearing the same confused look on his face, Ron directed this last question to the woman at the door.

Even as he answered the string of questions, he was trying to figure out where the police were going with their questions. Even to his own ears he knew his answers were now coming out with a slightly defensive attitude, surly almost. He wasn't trying to be coy or defensive, but when things didn't make sense . . .

"Did any one see you arrive today? Was any one else there in the house?" Detective Hubert asked as he continued to write in a small black notebook, glancing up quickly at Ron as he asked the question.

Ron tried his best to answer the questions clearly with no defensive tone. He knew that would not get him anywhere.

"Well, I did talk to Mr. Wells, her neighbour, outside on the sidewalk before I went in to her house. No one else was in the house, though. I already said she lives alone."

"The call to 911 didn't come from your aunts' house, why is that, Mr. Walker? If you thought she was hurt, why did you leave her alone in the house to make the call?"

This time Ron was defensive and he knew it. The questions were getting stranger by the minute.

"Look officer, my aunt doesn't have a phone, never has. Like I said, she's mute and can't talk to any one. I used Mr. Wells' phone next door, but I went right back to her house, you know, to try to help her. I told the operator that on the phone. I didn't know what else to do."

The frustration he felt at not knowing what was going on or what these officers wanted from him could be heard in his voice. He was becoming increasingly agitated and anxious at the same time. Try as he might, his mind could not come up with any explanation for these questions about his aunt or what interest she would hold for the police.

"Can't you just tell me what's going on? I'll answer all your questions, but . . ."

"Mr. Walker," Detective Hubert interrupted, "has your aunt ever indicated to you that someone might try, or has already tried, to hurt her?"

This question stopped Ron cold.

"What? That's crazy. What are you talking about? She's just an old lady who lives by herself. She rarely goes out anymore and as far as I know, only my mother and myself ever visit her. The only other person she ever sees is Mr. Wells from next door. He's as old as she is. Who would want to hurt her? Hurt her how, anyway? I thought maybe she had a heart attack or something. What are you trying to tell me? Are you saying someone broke in and did something to Aunt Edith?"

Now Ron was on his feet again, his voice rising in both pitch and timber. Even to himself, he sounded close to hysterical. He knew something was definitely wrong here, he just couldn't figure out what.

"Please, just calm down sir and have a seat. These questions are just a matter of routine. Part of our job is to investigate assaults, specifically, elder abuse. Your aunt has some, well, let's say, "irregular injuries", to quote the doctor. These injuries suggest someone has possibly hurt her, perhaps even on more than one occasion. We just need to figure out who she had contact with."

Detective Hubert finally sat opposite Ron as he spoke, gesturing him to sit as well. The other detective, who had still not made any comments, remained silently at the door. Both were looking at him as if he knew what they were talking about. They were, unfortunately, mistaken.

"Elder abuse? I don't understand. What kind of injuries are you talking about? Didn't she have a heart attack? I didn't see any injuries. There wasn't any blood on her or on the floor when the ambulance attendants moved her. Are you saying she was hurt on the way here? Can I go see her now? I need to call my mother to come here."

Ron sputtered as he sat, wringing his hands without realizing he was doing so. He knew he was not making any sense, but neither were the other two people in the room. Who had come into his aunts' house and hurt her? Had he scared the intruder away this morning when he knocked on the door?. What if he had not stopped to talk to Mr. Wells, what if he had just gone right in? All these thoughts ran through his head simultaneously.

"Mr. Walker, we don't think someone broke in or any thing like that. Nor was she hurt on the way here. If you'll let me explain, I think you'll better understand our concerns. Her injuries are rather strange to say the least. Your aunt has some marks on her back. By "marks" I mean straight cut lines. To me, and to her doctor, they look like whip marks, like maybe some one has whipped her on the back; lots of times actually and maybe for a long time, possibly years, judging by the scars. Do you know any thing about that?"

Now both detectives were looking at him closely, waiting for his reply and possibly his reaction to the news. What they saw was what was in his head, nothing. He stood with his mouth open slightly.

For a minute Ron didn't have a reply to give. His mind went blank. He couldn't understand what he was being told. He couldn't relate this information to his very passive, introverted old aunt.

Ron suddenly stood. "What the hell are you talking about? Why would any one want to hurt my aunt?"

He started to pace the room, feeling like a yoyo out of control. "I can tell you this; she lived by herself, kept to herself. She can't talk. She's just an old lady.

He stopped moving, standing to face the burly detective. "I'm sure that if she was being hurt, she would have let my mother or I know about it. None of this is making any sense to me." He muttered, as a look of both fear and confusion passed over his face. Both detectives waited patiently for him to finish what they knew he needed to say.

"I don't understand any of what you are saying. Are these marks on her back why she collapsed?" Ron looked from one to the other for an answer.

"Okay Sir, we understand you're confused. We're just here to try to figure this out. At the request of the hospital, we took a couple Polaroid's before we came in here, when we were in talking to the doctor. I'm going to show these to you now. I will warn you, though, they are pretty graphic and in my view, disturbing." Detective Hubert advised.

Detective Hubert slowly pulled two small square pictures from his well cut jacket pocket, looked at them briefly, and then handed them to Ron.

He looked at them in horror and disbelief, his face going white as a sheet as a wave of nausea came over him. He swallowed hard as he returned silently to the couch, unable to remain standing any longer.

"What does this look like to you, Mr. Walker? The doctor agreed with us that the marks look like some type of whip made them, but other than that, she doesn't know or want to venture as to an explanation without more information." Detective Hubert stated as he bent forward to point out a particular area in the photo.

"A whip? You're telling me someone used a whip on Edith? What in god's name for?" The question came out quietly, any defensiveness now gone from his voice.

"Yes, Mr. Walker, we think a whip. Some of the marks you'll see are definitely healed, but others are fairly open and fresh. We need your help here to figure this out."

Ron stared at the two photos, turning them around, trying to figure out what he was looking at. Out of habit, he turned them over but saw only the black back of a Polaroid. Reluctantly he turned then face up.

From what he could tell, he was looking at a back, he recognized the bones of the spine running down the centre. He saw a head of grey hair pulled to one side, in order to expose the entire surface for the picture. There were stripes, some faded, some red and fresh. They varied in length, but for the most part he guessed each one to be about 15 to 20 centimetres long. He could not even begin to guess how many lines he was seeing; they were so inter mingled with each other. They criss-crossed each other, lying on top of each other, like the baskets woven of bamboo they had made one year as a child for mother's day.

He had never seen any thing like this on a person before, although he suddenly thought of the scene with the scissors in the waiting room. His mind didn't know what to make of what his eyes were seeing. All he could do was stare and try to comprehend, without success. Finally he handed the pictures back with a shaking hand and now a shaking head.

The room was spinning for Ron. It was suddenly very hot, too small and did not contain enough air. What the hell was going on? Suddenly he couldn't remain still any longer. His mind couldn't move but his body needed to.

He stood again, looking around the room that no longer seemed as cozy as it had when he had first entered. It now felt like a prison and he needed to escape the confines of the four walls, but more importantly, he needed to get away from those pictures.

"I have to go see my aunt," he suddenly blurted. He started toward the door, where the female detective remained standing. Now Ron could not remember her name.

"Wait, Mr. Walker, please. Let me talk to my partner for a moment if you will." Detective Hubert had made his way toward the door and his partner. They exited the room, closing the door behind them. Ron fell into the couch, unable to stand yet unable to sit. He could hear the two detectives outside the door, but not what they were saying. He no longer cared.

Outside the door, Hubert turned to his partner.

"What do you think, Jr.?" He had called her this ever since she had been a little girl. The two had known each other for many years. He'd been her father's partner for a number of years and they knew each other well.

"This guy doesn't know anything about those marks, Bear. Did you see the look on his face? I thought he was going to lose his cookies on your nice suit." O'Leary said with a grin.

Because they had known each other for many years, both on and off the force, she could be very straightforward with her senior partner. She also liked to call him Bear whenever she could. The nickname started when she was about five and he had tried to grow a beard. She told him he looked like a bear and the name had stuck, not just with her, but just about everyone at the station used the moniker as well. He had gotten used to it over the years and finally decided it was a good description of how he wanted to be perceived.

"Yeah, you're right about that," he agreed. "Regardless, it wouldn't hurt to get a look at her place, if we could." They returned to the room with a plan, which they had agreed she would present. They worked well as a team.

Ron looked up as the two entered the room. He waited expectantly for the questions to start again. For no logical reason, he was pleased when Detective O'Leary spoke to him.

"Mr. Walker, we'd like to go take a look around your aunt's home. Maybe we can find something there that will explain this. Since she is not in a position to give us permission, we're asking you." Detective O'Leary had approached Ron while she waited for his reply.

"You think you'll find something at her house? What could you possibly find that would explain this? No one except my aunt lives there, what do you think you would find?" Ron knew he was rambling but couldn't help himself.

"At this point we're not sure, but something has definitely happened to your aunt, wouldn't you agree? Do you want to help us find out what?" Detective O'Leary continued, taking a step forward. Her voice was calm and gentle as it reached Ron's ears. For just a moment, their eyes locked. He thought she was genuine in her desire to find out what had happened to his aunt and he knew he needed answers for himself.

Ron stood, trying to think, to determine what was needed here as well as what was expected of him. He wished his father were here. He would know exactly what to do.

"Okay, look, I don't understand any of this. Do you understand that? I don't know what to do. I'm sure there's no problem seeing inside her house, even though I know she wouldn't be happy with having people there. That's just the way she is." Ron shrugged, pausing to gather his thoughts as he ran his hand through his hair. He returned to the couch while deciding what to do.

"I'm also sure there's no one hiding out in the cellar or the attic, sneaking around the house at night with a whip. I'm just as sure there is nothing there to find to explain this. But I have the key; I brought it with me when I followed the ambulance. When do you want to see the house"? He directed his question to Detective O'Leary

The energy which had surged through his body a minute ago was gone, replaced by an empty space that he could not identify. His mind was swimming with late night B movies about werewolves and other strange beasts of the night. Crazy thoughts and he knew it. He absently ran his hand over the smooth fabric of the cushion.

Detective O'Leary now sat directly across from him on the arm of the matching chair. She spoke in a quiet and comforting voice.

"Let's start here with a bit of information, then you can go see your aunt, get hold of your mom or any one else that you think might like to come . . ."

Ron interrupted her. "There is no one else, just my mom and I and my aunt. My dad's gone."

"Okay, then what can you tell us about your aunt?"

"Edith doesn't have any children and I'm an only child, Detective. She's never had anyone except us. I don't even know who her friends might be, except maybe old Mr. Wells, I suppose. I was just going visiting . . ." Ron trailed off, not sure where his thought had been going.

"What kind of a woman is she?" Detective O'Leary gently asked.

"She's, well, a lonely person, I guess I would say.

"Does she go out much, groups, clubs, other social activities?"

She doesn't go out, except to her garden. She lives by herself. What else? She loves her garden. What can I tell you?" Ron stumbled.

"Has your aunt ever been married?"

"Um, yes, a long time ago, but her husband walked out on her long before my time. My mom told me that. Since then, she's lived by herself."

"Does she work?"

"She used to work at the old hotel on the highway, cleaning rooms, until it burned down. Since then she just stays home. I visit her on Saturdays and my mom drops in when she can. Does any of this really help"? Ron asked, looking at the two detectives searchingly. He really had no idea what they wanted to know.

"Everything helps, Mr. Walker, even if it doesn't seem important right now," said Detective Hubert in an almost gentle voice.

"I don't think there is any emergency, but can we meet you at your aunt's house in a couple hours? You said you have the key to get in, right?" Ron nodded yes to her question.

"So, we'll meet you there, but please, to help us in this investigation, don't go into the house until we arrive." Detective Hubert requested as he stood up from the chair he had taken, and tucked his notebook into his pocket. Clearly he was ready to go. Detective O'Leary stood as well, the interview was over.

Ron instinctively touched the key in his pocket he had grabbed on the way out.

"Yes, I can meet you to let you in the house. First, I have to call my mom, tell her about Aunt Edith. We thought she would be okay, so mom's waiting at home for me to call. I'm sure she's going to want to come down now. I can meet you at the house in a couple hours."

Ron stood himself, feeling anxious. He wanted to see both see his aunt and to talk to his mother about all this. He wished again it could be his father he would be talking to. His head was swimming and he felt like a drowning man in a rainstorm. Life had handed him a huge curve ball and he needed time to think about everything he had been told. Someone had been hurting Edith? Impossible. He had so many questions, he needed some answers and at this point he simply wasn't sure where they would come from.

Ron called his mother from the public pay phone in the waiting room and attempted to explain the situation as best he could.

"Mom, I'm still at the hospital. Something weird is going on though. Edith has these whip marks on her back and . . ."

"What are you talking about Ron? Slow down"

"Okay, sorry. I just spoke to two police officers . . ."

"What are the police doing there?"

"Mom, please, just listen for a minute, I'm trying to explain. They have Edith in intensive care and they took pictures of her back. I saw them myself. They're keeping her here but the police are wanting to see her place and are asking me what's going on. I don't know anything about this, do you?"

"Ron, it's okay. I'm sure this is all a mistake. She probably scraped her back taking some of her junk downstairs." She sounded like she was trying to convince herself as much as Ron.

"No, mom. This is no scrape. So you don't know anything about this?" Ron thought if his mother could see the pictures, she wouldn't be dismissing this so easily.

"No Ron, I don't know a thing. We both know Edith has always been a little off; she has a lot of strange behaviours."

"I know that mom, but who would want to hurt Edith?" Ron asked.

"We don't even know yet that that is what's going on. What do the police want exactly?" his mother responded, dismissing the concern Ron felt.

"Well, right now they want answers but they also want to see her house. I'm going to meet them there and let them in. Do you want to be there?" Ron asked hopefully.

"You go ahead Ron. I'll finish up what I'm doing here and when you're finished with the police we can go back to the hospital. I'm sure Edith will be able to tell us what's going on. How does that sound?"

"Fine I guess. I'll come over after the police leave." Ron was disappointed that his mother wouldn't attend and help answer questions from the police with him.

Just before she hung up, she said "Sometimes we never really know the people we think we know, Ron."

This seemed strange to Ron, but after the events of the day so far, he let it slide.

'Well, that didn't get me anywhere', Ron thought. He had hoped for a bit more help from his mother, something he could pass on to the police, but it looked like he was going in empty handed again.

Edith had been settled into a semi private room. She had been asleep and had not responded to him. He saw the tubes connected to her and the various machines beside her bed, but he had no idea what they were for. They all seemed to be working, so he decided that was a good thing. Having spent very little time at the hospital, all this was new to him.

With the machines, wires and tubes everywhere, all seeming to do a very important job, Ron could do nothing but look at her lying motionless on the bed. It struck him just how thin she was in her cotton hospital gown.

Aunt Edith? Aunt Edith, can you hear me? I'm right here if you need me." Ron spoke quietly to the sleeping form.

His aunt looked asleep, but he spoke to her anyway, hoping she could hear him and understand that he was there. He stroked her hair gently. He waited a few minutes, but still she did not respond.

Aunt Edith, I have to leave now but mom and I will be back later. You rest now and I'll see you soon." He kissed her forehead and left the room.

Ron spoke to the nurse briefly to see if he could find out anything else. The nurse confirmed his aunt was not well; she had indeed had a heart attack, but there were other complications.

"I'm sorry but we don't know anything else right now. You'll have to wait to speak to the attending physician, Dr Main," he was told.

The exact nature of these 'complications' she would not explain, She did say that his aunt was in very serious condition, and would be remaining under the care of the Intensive Care Unit staff for the time being.

It seemed to Ron, based on his interactions so far at the hospital that the nurse was suggesting it would be more than just Edith they would be watching, but maybe he was just being paranoid now. After all, why would the nurse think she needed to keep an eye on him? He felt ridiculous for even thinking something like that.

He decided she was just tired from a long shift of caring for sick people. He smiled at her and thanked her for looking after his aunt.

He tried again to gather any information he could pass on to his mother. The nurse maintained she couldn't, or maybe wouldn't, tell him what those other complications were that she had mentioned. She would only say that he would need to speak to the doctor when she came back to the floor. Ron felt that the nurse was not pleased to have him there and wanted him to leave as soon as possible, even though he knew this was ridiculous.

Ron finally decided he was not just paranoid. Her careful scrutiny of him told him everything he needed to know, except why this nurse had taken such a dislike to him for no reason. She remained in the room during Ron's entire visit with his aunt. She fiddled with various items but at the same time he felt she was watching his every move and listening closely to everything he said to Edith. It soon dawned on him that, for some reason, this woman thought he was somehow responsible for hurting his aunt. Being there now made him very uncomfortable.

Chapter 4

Ron left the hospital to keep his appointment with the police. He had plenty of time before the two detectives would arrive there, so he decided to walk the 12 blocks from the hospital instead of calling for another cab. He needed the fresh air to think about all that had just happened. He desperately needed to get his head cleared. The police had asked him to wait for them before going back into his aunt's home and he had agreed to that. He was not anxious right now anyway to go wandering through the house on his own. He didn't think they are going to find anything, and yet, who knew? He left the hospital more confused than he had ever been in his entire life.

Ron walked slowly toward his destination. Each step taking him in the right direction while his mind wandered it's own path. His feet shuffled along the sidewalk, his hands stuffed into the pockets of his track pants. To those around him who had observed him leave the hospital, the tall young man looked troubled.

He had known his aunt his whole life, or at least until today, he thought he had. He didn't dislike his aunt; no, nothing like that. It was more like, she had scared him a little when he had been young with her soundless way of communicating. He knew she couldn't talk, but it used to seem really weird to him. He had wanted to "talk all the time", as his father used to remind him.

Sometimes when he had been young, just for fun, he would try not to say any thing during the whole time he was there. He just wanted to see what it was like, but he could never do it. He had not been able to understand how she could just not talk.

He had spent a lot of time as a child thinking about this and wondering what that would be like. As he had grown older and possibly more mature, he still wondered why someone would not talk. He had not figured out an answer for that either but had come to accept that that was his aunt.

Now, he learned to do what his mother had done when they visited together. He would chat with his aunt, tell her about himself, what he had been up to, at school, and with his friends. He knew she enjoyed this time; she would sit quietly, nodding her head and smiling during his monologue. This seemed to be what she really wanted to know about, what she would show an interest in. On occasion she would grab a book from the table and write down a question or comment on what he had been saying. He would stop his chatter and answer the question or clarify what she wanted to know. It was a strange way to have a conversation. But by the time he had started visiting on his own, he didn't really think it was so strange after all.

At times through out his life, he had also always wondered why she had never learned to use sign language.

"Hey Mr., got any spare change"? The scraggly man stood directly in front of him. Ron stopped short, his heart suddenly beating faster as he was brought back to the present. Ron realized the dirty man must have come out from the alley between the two buildings.

"What?" Ron muttered disoriented at the interruption of his thoughts of the past. Ron realized he had been concentrating on his own thoughts so intently that he had not really heard what the guy had said. For a minute he was afraid, not knowing what the guy in the dirty clothes wanted from him. Ron glanced quickly around to see where he might get help if he needed it.

"Sorry. What did you say"? Ron stuttered again.

"Hey man, I just need some change for coffee. You got any or not?" The stranger held out his hand, which was covered in a dirty glove. Clearly he was expecting something would be given to him.

Ron could smell the sour odour coming from the man in front of him. A mixture of old cheap wine and unwashed sweat permeated the man and rolled over Ron in a rush.

"C'mom man. The Mission don't open for another two hours. Just a bit of change for a cup a'java. What d'ya say"? The bum swayed from side to side, as he took a step closer, his unsteady hand reaching toward Ron.

Instinctively, Ron stepped back, away from both the man and the terrible smell coming from him. His nose wrinkled at the odour

He thought it was unlikely this stranger had any plans to buy a cup of coffee. The man had spent too many nights in the dirty alley, too many days without a shower or a change of clothes to be worried about coffee, Ron felt certain.

Ron wondered briefly what the man would do in the winter, in January say, when the wind blew and the snow fell in the minus 40-degree air. Just as quickly he dismissed his concern. Ron had his own problems to deal with and, like most people, didn't spend much time worrying about the homeless people in the area.

Trying not to stare or breath too deeply Ron reached into his pocket. He pulled out a couple of Toonies and various other small coins. He handed them over without even looking at what had been in his pocket. He didn't usually give money to the street people, preferring instead, again like most people, to cross the street in order to avoid them. Today he had been caught off guard and didn't want to get into an argument here on the street.

The guys' dirty face lit up when the change clinked into his hand, his dirty glove closing over the money protectively. In a flash he was gone, to where Ron could not say, leaving Ron, thankfully, standing on the sidewalk alone.

He shook his head to clear it and bring himself back into focus. He resumed his walk, quickening his pace, wanting to get to the house.

"What will I find there"? Ron mused out loud. He couldn't help but wonder if he would have more questions than answers by the days end. Today, anything seemed possible. Right now it seemed impossible to believe he could be any more confused than at this moment.

As his feet started to move, images of the photos he had seen at the hospital flooded his brain. All Ron could think of were pictures he had seen in books of the African-American slaves who had been beaten into submission by their sadistic white owners. He had seen whippings in movies, but of course these weren't real, but the marks the whip left seemed the same as what had been on Edith's back.

"This makes no sense," Rom mumbled, yet the images continued. Flashes of Jesus, fallen to the ground during his long trek in 'Passion of the Christ' also came to mind. His bloody and whipped body lying in the dirt, the cross hatch of welts growing as the whips continued to be applied to his back. But Edith was not a religious figure being persecuted for her convictions.

Ridiculous thoughts, Ron decided. None of that explained the marks he had seen. Even if someone had punished her in this way in the past, Ron thought, some of the marks he had seen had clearly been fresh. Red and welted areas on the skin of her back, over powering the older healed scars from who knew how long ago.

How long could this have been going on? How is it no one had ever known? Why, Ron wondered, had his aunt not said anything or asked for help from her family?

Suddenly the squealing of tires and the blare of a horn brought Ron back to reality. A car had braked, stopping just inches from him. His mind barely registered some one yelling behind him. "Look out". At the same time, Ron felt a hand on his shoulder, stopping him in mid-stride.

He hadn't even realized he had stepped out into the intersection, and had almost been hit by a car. The driver yelled something unintelligible out the window and swerved around him. Staring at the passing car, Ron saw the driver give him the finger in the mirror as the horn blared.

Hey Mr. That was close. Are you okay"? A man's voice came from behind.

"Yes, thanks. I guess I've been day dreaming." Ron absently pushed his hair back from his face, remembering vaguely he had planned to get a hair cut this afternoon. Obviously that was going to have to wait, he thought. It looked like all his plans would have to wait for the time being. Ron stepped back to the sidewalk and took a deep breath.

"Okay man, pull yourself together. Just get home and figure this out in the safety of the house." Ron shook his head and muttered under his breath. People waiting at the light looked at him, moving a step or two away as he mumbled to himself.

When the light changed, he walked quickly but remained very alert the rest of the way. Nothing would be gained if he ended up in a hospital bed beside his aunt. Nervousness wracked his body. Did the police or the Dr think he had done something to Edith? Is that why they had spoken to him? Is that why they wanted to see the house?

Although he was not 100% certain they were placing the blame on him for Edith's injuries, that feeling would just not go away. Perhaps they were just being cautious, making sure his aunt stayed safe. With regards to that piece of the puzzle, it would need to be sorted out once Edith woke up and could reassure the hospital staff and the police that her nephew had not harmed her in any way.

When Ron finally arrived at the house, with fortunately, no further mishaps, Mr. Wells was still outside. Moving his broom from side to side along the sidewalk, Ron noticed him looking up often towards the road, squinting into the sun. Interest in the leaves seemed to be gone. Ron thought he probably hadn't left the sidewalk since the ambulance had raced away, unless he had gone inside to give an updated report to his wife, which was always possible.

"How is she, son?" Mr. Wells inquired eagerly when Ron reached the house. The broom stopped moving now as the old man leaned heavily on it.

"Not good, I'm afraid, Mr. Wells." Ron said as he stopped directly in front of the man.

"The Doctor said she's had a heart attack. She's in ICU right now. I'm not sure of any thing else just yet. She is sleeping, which I guess is best." Mr. Wells nodded and listened to Ron intently.

"I tried to clean the leaves on her steps for her, but it looks like they've all returned. I can try again if you want," Mr. Wells said.

"No, it's okay. I'll take care of that. Thanks anyway." Ron glanced towards the steps as both men stood in silence.

"Mr. Wells, do you know . . . , well, what I mean is, did my aunt have any visitors? Did you see people coming and going from her house?"

Since Mr. Wells was always here, either sitting in the window or sweeping up the walk, he probably knew more about what went on in the neighbourhood than any one else. Ron felt he had to at least try to find out anything that might provide some answers and understanding. Mr. Wells seemed like a good place to start.

"Visitors? Why yes son, I see you every weekend, sometimes I see your mom come by. How is your mom anyway?"

"My mom? Oh, she's fine. But Mr. Wells, what about other visitors?" Keeping the old man on track was frustrating for Ron at this moment.

"Oh, right, visitors. Well, Mrs. Wells visits when she can. Mind you, her health is not what it used to be, so she doesn't get out as often as she used to." Mr Wells glanced at the window. Ron waited, hoping he would get to someone alive.

"Those two still spend plenty of time talking over the back fence in the warmer weather, but the flowers are gone now, so there's not as much to do out there these days. Edith and Liz always did get along and enjoy sharing their flower cuttings and garden secrets, as I'm sure you know. Why don't you ask her if your aunt had other friends? Women share those kinds of things with each other." His voice softened when he spoke of his wife.

It seemed everyone but Mr. Wells knew she was dead. Ron briefly wondered if he knew but just didn't want to admit it. The rest of his faculties seemed to be intact.

Ron was pretty sure neither the police nor himself would be talking to the woman any time soon or that she was going to be of much help even if the police decided to ask her questions. Ron was certain her head stone would not respond, even if it were the police standing there beside the daisies, trying to ferret out the "women's secrets" she may have had knowledge of.

Ron was mildly disappointed but not surprised. He hadn't so far learned anything from the one source he thought might be able to help. He decided he had been expecting to find easy answers to a very difficult situation. Maybe the police were right. There might be answers in the house that Ron had never been aware of. He was both nervous and excited at the same time as he waited for their arrival.

"Well, thanks, Mr. Wells. I'll get back to you about that" Ron said.

Both men looked over at the road as a car pulled up to the curb and stopped. The two detectives from the hospital exited the vehicle at the same time.

"Mr. Wells, I have to go now and speak to these people. I'll let you know how Aunt Edith is doing after I go back to the hospital. Thanks for letting me use your phone earlier." Ron turned to greet his company.

"Hi," Ron walked toward the two officers. "I just arrived. I haven't been inside." He stopped about two feet from the two.

"Thanks for meeting us, Mr. Walker." The big man said. Ron looked toward his partner, but she didn't respond.

"That's Mr. Wells over there. He's lived here as long as I can remember. I talked to him while I was waiting for you. He says the only visitor Aunt Edith ever has is my mom, his wife and myself. He knows the neighbourhood and the people in it. He didn't know who else may have been visiting with her." Ron felt it was important to share the little information he had gathered so far even though he knew it was nothing and that he was rambling nervously. He hoped he wasn't sweating. Wasn't that a sign of guilt of something?

"Well, after we look through the house, maybe we should speak to his wife. She might know more than he does, you know, girl talk, something she didn't think was important before. The old girls may have talked about what ever is going on." Detective Hubert said to his partner, who nodded in silent agreement but rolled her eyes at her partner. Ron decided she wasn't much of a talker.

Before they spent too much time developing a plan that would involve interviewing the corpse of Mrs. Wells for all her secrets, Ron thought he had better share one other piece of information.

"That's probably not a very good or practical idea, Detectives." Ron directed this to Detective O'Leary.

"Mrs. Wells certainly had been a very good friend and neighbour to my aunt ever since I can remember. Unfortunately she has been dead for the last couple years."

The two detectives exchanged a look that Ron did not understand. Neither commented on this information.

"Mr. Wells doesn't want to deal with that, I guess."

"He always talks like she is just inside, waiting to feed me home made chocolate cookies with coconut and milk like she used to when I was a kid." Ron smiled at the memory.

"Before she died, she was very sick. She had cancer throughout her body and was pretty well confined to her bed for the last year she was alive." Again the looked passed between the partners. This time Ron recognized it. They knew there were no answers to be found from Mrs. Wells.

Ron nervously continued. "Before that, she spent a lot of time either at the hospital for treatments or sitting in her front window watching Mr. Wells on the sidewalk. I doubt she and Aunt Edith shared many secrets in the last five years or so." Ron took the key from his pocket and turned towards the steps, still trying to explain Mrs. Wells.

"I know they used to spend a lot of time together in their gardens when she was alive; sharing seeds, cuttings, gardening tips, stuff like that. Mr. Wells lives in his own world and that seems to work for him, but I don't think it will be much help to you."

He started up the stairs with both officers following him.

"Well. I guess that happens sometimes to old people." Detective O'Leary commented from behind him. To Ron's ears her voice was both confident but understanding at the same time.

He opened the door to the dingy hallway. Even though the bright afternoon sun was streaming through the open front door, the over head light was needed to brighten to space. Ron flicked the switch as he passed, allowing the others to enter.

The old dirty colour of the painted walls didn't help either, Ron knew. The years of accumulated dirt were added to the look of disrepair. The curtains were closed everywhere in the house, shutting out the outside world, not inviting in any unwanted company. It had always been this way. Ron was sure of his initial doubt about finding any clues in this house. His aunt had once written that she didn't like people knowing her business unless she chose to share it.

"I guess your aunt didn't care for the sunshine," Detective O'Leary commented when they had gathered in the hall. Ron smiled at her, knowing she was tying to be kind.

Ron had been trying to get Edith to open the curtains, maybe even the windows, to let the nice summer air in for years. He had not been successful. Ron, the exact opposite of the old woman, rarely had the curtains at his own small apartment closed. He preferred the natural light as much as possible. This was another reason he liked the other seasons more than winter, the loss of daylight always made him feel like he was missing out on something important.

Detective Hubert walked into the living room behind Ron, looking around quickly, seeming to Ron to be taking everything in. Detective O'Leary entered the room last.

"Okay Mr. Walker, if it's okay with you, we'll take it from here." Detective Hubert's voice boomed in the quiet house.

"Sure, what ever you want" Ron agreed. What else was he supposed to do, he wondered?

"Could you please just sit here on the couch and wait while we have a look around? The big man gestured towards the single couch in the room.

"Do you want me to show you around or anything?" Ron asked tentatively.

"If we need you, we'll let you know. You said your aunt lived alone, is that right"? Detective Hubert moved toward the hall, planning to leave the room and Ron.

"Yes, that's right. She always has. I've never seen another person here when I've visited, besides my mom of course." Ron replied.

"Did your aunt own this house, Mr. Walker"? Detective O'Leary asked from behind him. Ron jumped slightly at the unexpected voice from behind him. Her lilting voice immediately put him at ease.

"I guess so. At least that's what I always thought. She's always lived here though." Ron knew he was babbling again. This woman made him both nervous and excited at the same time. Ridiculous, he thought to himself. She's here doing a job.

Ron sat and tried to make himself comfortable on the familiar couch. He waited to see what would be expected of him. The two detectives walked carefully around the room, being careful not to disturb the piles of stuff everywhere. Every few feet they returned their gaze to the shelves piled high with notebooks, paperbacks and magazines. There seemed to be no rhyme or reason to the organization. Ron knew there were books from gardening to romance and anything else in between. While Ron loved to read himself, he could not imagine having this many books or magazines at the same time in his home and covering so many topics.

"What are all the little notebooks for?" Detective O'Leary asked Ron, pointing at the shelves piled high with various sizes and colours of notebooks.

"Oh, she uses those when she was talking to someone. Sometimes she wrote in them as well, things about her garden, lists for the store, stuff like that.

"All those books? Why did she keep them all?"

"My aunt wrote things down, that was her life.

"Have you looked through these books yourself"? Detective O'Leary asked Ron. Her voice seemed hopeful.

"No, Sorry. I've never really looked at them beyond the one she would be writing in when I would visit. She always had one with her. I guess like a diary or something." Ron said as he continued to look at the Detective.

"This one on the coffee table is probably the most recent."

Ron picked up a small green notebook from the table in front of him and opened it to the first page.

"See, she writes about what is happening." He said as he flipped through the small black book.

"Here, she's talking about the excessive noise from some kids on the street one evening. I guess it was before school started for the year because she says school start soon and maybe parents will keep a better eye on their kids." Ron smiled as he read the complaint, imagining his aunt sitting here writing this down so she could discuss this with Ron when he came to visit.

"What about dates? Are the entries dated in any way?" Detective Hubert interrupted his thoughts.

"I don't think she generally put any dates down, nothing that I can see anyway." Ron started to turn the page when Detective Hubert reached out and quickly took the book from his hand.

The big man's hand covered the entire book. At just over six feet, Ron had never considered himself a small man until today.

"Maybe we better have a look at this first. It might have some information in it. You said like a diary, right?" He flipped quickly through the pages. "Okay, here is today or yesterday I guess, because it's the last entry." He read through it silently, and then looked up at Ron.

"She's writing about you, I guess. Says you'll be coming by today for a visit. Your name's Ronny, right?"

"Yes, but no one has called me Ronny since I was 10, just Ron." He smiled shyly at Detective O'Leary, feeling like a kid again in her presence.

"Well, Ron, it looks like your aunt still does. It also seems she was pretty happy you were coming to see her today. She wrote 'Ronny will be here soon, I love his visits, he always has so many things to tell me. He promised to bring some of that oatmeal bread I really like. He's a good boy, my Ronny. Maybe today he will tell me he has a new girlfriend. That last one did him no good. He can do better than that.' The two detectives glanced at each other, then back at Ron.

"She didn't like your girlfriend?" Detective Hubert asked, glancing up suspiciously from the little book he held.

"Well, she's never actually met her. We're not dating anymore. I talked to my aunt about her, of course, while we were dating, but she never wanted me to bring Laura around." Ron didn't know what else they wanted to know. The detectives stood in silence.

"She didn't like meeting new people. Last spring, after Laura and I broke up . . . well, I guess maybe I said some unfair things about her to my aunt."

Ron appeared to blush at this confession. He tried to look at only Detective Hubert and not at Detective O'Leary. He wasn't sure why.

"I was angry that she dumped me. She really was a nice person. Stupid, eh?"

Neither detective commented, but Detective O'Leary seemed to Ron to be smirking. Detective Hubert laid the book back on the table where it had been. Clearly the answers to this mystery were not contained in those pages.

"Okay, O'Leary, let's search the whole house first, then if we don't find anything, we'll have to look through all these books." He was careful to use her name and not her nickname when speaking in front of civilians and for that she was grateful.

He swung his arm in a circle, pointing to all the books that filled the bookcases and boxes piled around the room. The idea did not seem to appeal to either detective as they glanced at the collection. There were a lot of writing books stored here along with the novels and magazines she loved to read. Going through them would take hours.

Ron remained seated as the two detectives put on gloves. After that confession about his last girlfriend, he was embarrassed to say any thing else.

Cindy LaChance

"Okay, Mr. Walker, like I said, you stay here. We'll take a look through the house." The two detectives went toward the kitchen at the far end of the hall.

Ron sat and listened to the sounds of the strangers making their way through his aunt's house. He wanted to go with them, to help look for any thing that might explain the entire situation. He knew Edith would be very upset by this, people in her house she didn't know. He guessed he would have to deal with this when she got home. For now, it was more important to try to figure things out.

Besides, Ron thought, these were police and he could hardly tell them to get out, now could he?

He gazed absently around the room, thinking, not for the first time, just how lonely a woman his aunt must be. There were no family pictures on the walls, no television in the room to keep her company, probably not one in the whole house, as far as he knew. He recalled when he had offered to buy her a TV several years ago. She had smiled at him, shaking her head and informed him, with the help of her notebook and her loopy handwriting, that she had no interest in the things they showed on TV. She said she had seen enough at work, in the motel, and didn't want that type of noise intruding on her quiet home.

He had bought her a radio instead, which he could see sitting on a shelf between the books, but could not recall ever hearing it turned on when he had been here. He had seen the radio on the shelf during many visits and was secretly pleased that she at least had accepted this gift. He walked over to the radio and saw, as he looked closely, that it was not even plugged in. No wonder he had never heard it playing, he thought.

He had no real idea of how his aunt spent her time, except for her garden out back, of course. During the spring, summer and fall she spent a lot of time there, tending to and growing the flowers and vegetables that every year brought her so much joy.

Her roses were her pride and joy. Ron doubted roses at the Royal Botanical Gardens received any better care. She cared also for the honeysuckle and peonies, which grew along the fence and the pansies and marigolds under the trees, but her roses received daily tender care under her careful, loving hand.

Ron remembered many Saturday visits having been spent in this garden, planting, weeding, sometimes pulling off the dead leaves from the flowers, or harvesting the beets, beans, tomatoes and cucumbers she loved to grow in the small garden plot. He remembered as well many fall days spent right here in her kitchen, packing and canning those same vegetables he had helped plant, weed and pick with her during his visits; the pears from the trees as well were preserved for later use. It had always seemed to him that together, the two of them canned more than one person could ever eat, but . . .

"Mr. Walker, there's a bag of groceries spilled out there on the kitchen floor. Had your aunt been out shopping earlier, do you know?"

Detective O'Leary had come back into the living room alone, startling him from his thoughts. He noticed, though not for the first time, just how attractive she was. With her dark hair pulled back from her face, her brown eyes became the focus of her round face. The lack of make up did not detract from her natural beauty. Briefly Ron thought that if he had met her somewhere else, he would not imagine her as a cop, although he didn't know what a cop should look like.

He turned from the shelf when he heard her.

"Um, no, I brought those," he said. "I forgot to tell you about that. I'll go pick that up. I wasn't thinking about the mess when I left earlier."

Ron headed to the kitchen; no one tried to stop him. He noticed as he passed Detective O'Leary that she was nearly as tall as himself.

Detective Hubert was there, standing in the middle of the room and Detective O'Leary followed behind Ron.

"Your aunt sure did like to keep things, didn't she," he said as Ron reached for the bag. Detective Hubert swept his arm around at the open shelves in the kitchen. They were cluttered with cooking items and canned goods along with small knick-knacks that Ron had not noticed in a long time, if he ever really had. There were also more magazines piled on the chairs.

Ron smiled at this. "My mom used to try to talk her into having a garage sale, or a dump sale, as mom called it, but Aunt Edith never would agree. Yes, she liked to keep things."

Detective O'Leary had picked up several items from the floor and handed them now to Ron.

"Thanks" Ron smiled at her, turning to the counter. He put the items away as best he could in the crowded cupboards and over stocked fridge.

As he picked up the carton of eggs, she quickly placed her hand under his to prevent the broken eggs from escaping. He looked at her and smiled, both laughing at the same time. He threw into the garbage, making a mental note to take this outside before he left. Outside, they could hear the last birds of the season in the yard.

"Since I'm here, do you want me to make you some coffee? It might help to take the chill off. Aunt Edith never keeps the heat very high in here, not even in the dead of winter." The detectives looked at each other and both shook their heads no.

"Just go sit and wait for us in the other room, if you wouldn't mind. We're going to have a look upstairs, and then we'll come talk to you. If we have any more questions, we'll come ask." Detective Hubert stated, without turning around from the cupboard he was looking through.

Ron could tell the larger detective had dismissed him from the search, although his manner did not seem to be as aggressive as at the hospital. He returned to the living room alone, waiting to be called on again to answer whatever trivial questions they could think of. Not, he realized, that he would likely know the answers.

It wasn't long before Ron heard his name being called from the second storey; Detective O'Leary was calling to ask him to come upstairs with them. He was pleased and scared at the same time, not knowing what to expect when he reached the top. Ron moved as fast as he could, thinking they must have found something.

The bare wood steps were cluttered with more papers, flyers and old mail, like she just dropped everything here when the mailman brought it. He climbed carefully, making sure not to disturb the items and send everything like dominoes crashing to the front entrance below.

In the upper hall, both detectives were standing near a door in the dim hall. The one window on the landing, not surprisingly, covered with a dark blue curtain from top to bottom, preventing much light from entering, making it hard to see. Even with the limited light, it immediately occurred to Ron that the entire hallway was clear of clutter. He had no time to think about what this meant.

"Mr. Walker, would you say your Aunt is a religious woman? By that, I mean, did she attend any organized religious activities that you are aware of?" Detective Hubert asked as soon as Ron's feet hit the hallway floor.

"Religious? No, I don't think . . ."

"What about cult involvement? Would she be involved in anything like that?" Detective Hubert asked before Ron had even finished his last reply.

"Of course not. That's ridiculous. Why? What's going on? What have you found"? Ron asked as he moved slowly toward the door where the two detectives waited.

"Well, we found something a little strange. If you would, please don't touch any thing inside for now, but can you explain this?" Detective O'Leary asked as she opened the door. They had already turned on the overhead light in the room to break through the filtered grey light.

As Ron stood in the doorway he could see that it was a very clean and sparsely furnished bedroom. He saw a double sized bed centered to the wall directly under the window; it had been made up with perfect corners, not a wrinkle anywhere. A heavy green bedspread covered the bed. In contrast, a light white and pink nightgown lay folded neatly on the pillow, with matching slippers sitting side by side on the floor. Ron recognized these items as a gift from his mother the previous Christmas. He also saw a wooden night table on top of which sat a lamp with an empty water glass beside it. Heavy dark matching green curtains hung on the window and these were, of course, closed, preventing the sun from entering the room.

He felt like he had stepped into some one else's home, the room was so well kept. Fragments of 'Alice in Wonderland' flashed through his mind. Two worlds were colliding in a single second in Ron's mind. Chaos and organization separated by a single floor. Any second he expected a rabbit to come bounding by to tell him he was late, or possibly invite him to a tea party.

Ron was about to make a joke about this to the two other occupants in the room when he happened to glance to the right of the window, where a real looking glass actually stood. It was then he stopped. Stopped speaking, stopped thinking, almost stopped breathing.

The heavily decorated ornate mirror was at least five feet tall, trimmed in the same dark wood as the night table. Like any other dressing mirror, it had been placed close to the floor. A multi coloured mat had been placed neatly in front of it. Ron instinctively knew something was out of place, besides the ordered room, but his over burdened mind could not immediately comprehend what it was.

Without realizing he was doing so, Ron stepped further into the room until he felt a hand being placed gently on his shoulder. That stopped him. He turned at the touch and looked questioningly into the face of Detective O'Leary, still not understanding what this room contained or for that matter what it meant to every one in the room and his Aunt as well.

"You better not get any closer, Mr. Walker, until we know what we're dealing with here," she said quietly.

"Do you know what this is?" She asked as she pointed to the mirror.

Ron continued to look at her, his eyes begging for an explanation, any explanation; wanting her to help him comprehend and make sense of this room and this whole day. Slowly he turned back, not wanting to see, but having to in order to understand.

When he was able to focus and take everything in, he saw on the floor, leaning against the big mirror, a simple framed picture he had not seen before. There were three people in the picture, but he could not see who they were. The mirror, the mat and the picture were all spattered with red and brown. At first he didn't know what it was, then realized it must be blood.

For the first time Ron saw the whip as well, sitting innocently on the edge of the mat. The whip appeared to be made of strips of dark leather with a handle about two feet long. This too was covered with the dark brown of what could only be dried blood.

"What the hell is that?" he exclaimed.

"That looks like blood. What does this mean? What the hell's going on here?" He turned again to Detective O'Leary, shaking his head, scared, but also hoping she could answer any or all of his questions.

He felt dizzy all of a sudden. The room was spinning and he couldn't stop it. He took a step back and leaned against the doorframe, closing his eyes, trying to process this information. Willing himself not to be sick to his stomach at the same time.

"Mr. Walker, is it possible that your Aunt caused her own injuries by using that whip on herself? Do you recognize the people in the picture?" Detective Hubert had stepped further into the room, glancing at the picture, then back at Ron.

Ron took several deep breaths, keeping his eyes closed while he did so, trying to stay focused. He could feel his stomach churning. He could hear the questions but was unable to immediately respond. When he was ready, when the deep breaths had calmed his heart rate and his stomach enough, he opened his eyes.

"I'll need to get closer to see the picture," he said quietly. "I can barely make out that there are three people, let alone who they might be."

"Okay, go easy and sit on this side of the bed, don't touch anything though," Detective O'Leary said, placing her hand at his elbow to guide him forward toward the bed.

Ron felt her touch and was glad that she was there helping him with this. For an instant he wondered if she were single, then thought, where did that come from? His mind returned to the task at hand.

He slowly moved as close as the police would let him, sitting on the edge of the carefully made bed, feeling like Alice after falling down the rabbit hole into a world he knew nothing about. He stared hard at the picture, trying to make himself see the people in it, beyond the spattering of blood on the picture frame. The people preserved behind the glass had been wiped clean of any spatters, the contrast obvious, even to Ron. The picture was clearly old and had been processed in black and white. It showed a man with two children. They appeared posed; as if the picture had been taken after everyone had been set up just right by the photographer. The man looked to be about 30 or so, he was smiling for the camera, his thick black hair cut neatly short. He was dressed formally in a dark suit and tie, which did not appear to be a natural costume for him. Although he couldn't say why, to Ron, he looked more like the kind of man who would wear much more casual clothes. Ron was not sure why he thought that, but it popped into his head none-the less.

The two children sat on the man's lap; two small children, one swaddled in a blanket with just the small cherub of a face showing, the other being held tightly, possessively, as if he could not yet sit unattended or perhaps wouldn't sit still if released. The older one was looking straight ahead into the camera, a happy smile on his face. Ron guessed this one to be a boy, not because he knew or could really tell, but just because of the outfit, a white shirt and pants and a small hat perched on his head.

Ron wondered briefly how any one could get a child so little to sit so still like that for a picture. He studied the faces, trying to figure out who they could be; something seemed familiar to him but he could not say what. The longer he looked, the more he became convinced that he didn't know who those people were.

"You said your aunt had been married for a time until her husband left her. Do you know if she had any children? Could this be her family?"

Ron jumped at the sound of Detective O'Leary's voice from his right, bringing him back to the present.

"No, she didn't have any children. I don't know who these people are. None of this makes any sense to me," Ron paused, still looking at the detective. "Are you thinking my Aunt hurt herself, on purpose, like those religious fanatics who go around whipping themselves to atone for some perceived or imagined sin, because they believe God told them to?"

It was all he could think of. Ron's head was still spinning; he couldn't keep his thoughts straight. Neither detective responded to the idea.

"What could my aunt possibly have done to make her think that way? She's a good person. She's not religious; at least I don't think so. She never even went to church as far as I know. She never talked about religion . . ." Ron trailed off, still staring at the picture, still trying to figure out what all this meant.

Detective O'Leary gently took Ron's elbow to help him up. She started to lead him away from the bed and the unsettling scene. They moved together toward the door. Ron was glad she was there.

"Come on, Mr. Walker. Let's all go down stairs and think this through. I'm sure there is some explanation. It might be easier if we're away from here." Her voice was gentle and soothing. For that Ron was grateful once again.

With Detective O'Leary's hand still on his arm, Ron allowed himself to be led down the stairs and back to the familiar chaos of the living room. He collapsed onto the couch, staring straight ahead, no longer seeing anything the room contained. The three remained quiet, each lost in thoughts of their own about what they had just witnessed on the second floor.

Suddenly Ron needed to bring in the outside light. He felt entombed, claustrophobic.

"I need to open the curtains," he said to no one in particular, as he jumped up and walked to the front window.

"I need day light. I can't stand this dark dreariness."

Ron grabbed the edges of the fabric and pulled back the curtains in both windows, the dust which had gathered on the unused curtains for so long swirling around him. Ron didn't care; his efforts were rewarded by the steams of light flooding in, showing more than before the contrast between the order in the upstairs bedroom and the clutter that encompassed the main floor of the house.

While everyone was gathering their thoughts, the silence enveloped the room. A trilling sound suddenly filled the room, making Ron jump, although he did not know why. He certainly had no reason to be nervous about being in a house he had been in for most of his life. Detective Hubert reached for his belt and pulled out his pager that had been hooked there.

"It's the hospital," he announced, after looking at the box he held in his hand. "Can I use the phone?" he asked Ron.

"There isn't one here. I already told you that my aunt is mute so she never had one installed" Ron snapped back in response, not caring any longer how he sounded. Just trying to make sense of all that had occurred was more than he could manage, social graces would have to wait.

"Right. Sorry. I forgot. I'll go out to the car," he said to his partner as he headed out the door.

Ron looked at Detective O'Leary, who had remained standing by the bookcase. She was looking around the room again.

"What does all this mean? Does it make any sense to you?" he asked, as he returned slowly to the couch and sank heavily into the cushions. Now that the curtains were open, he could see the dust motes swirling through the air around him. This, he thought, was the least of his worries.

"To be honest, I'm as confused as you are. I've never seen a situation like this before. When we initially saw her injuries, we assumed some one had purposely hurt your aunt. That's why the hospital called us in after they saw all those marks on her back. They thought abuse and we agreed. Now, after seeing her room, it looks like maybe she could have done this to herself. I'm guessing here, but possibly she was punishing herself for some unknown reason by whipping her back upstairs in that bedroom. I can't think of any other explanation for her injuries. Has she ever said anything to you, or your mother, that would suggest something like this?" Detective O'Leary sat in the chair across from Ron, appearing as perplexed as he was feeling.

Ron shook his head, not knowing what to say. He believed this woman was as confused and surprised by what they had found as he was. He could see the questions in her eyes, and the confusion about what they had just seen upstairs on her face. She seemed to be trying to make sense of this as much as he was. He continued to look at her, thinking that he really did like looking at her and again being struck by her as a person.

"I guess we'll have to ask her when she's feeling better," was all he was able to come up with. They sat in silence until her partner returned.

"Mr. Walker, the hospital says your Aunt has had a turn for the worse. They obviously can't get hold of you. I think we had better go back there now." Detective Hubert said as he returned to the room.

"What do you mean, a turn for the worse? Is she okay?" Ron asked as he stood up, too quickly. The blood once again rushed to his head. The dizziness he had felt before returned again. There was simply too much happening too fast.

"Can we go get my mother?" he stuttered. "She's not well herself, but she'll want to be there if her only sister's not doing well."

"I'll radio in for a patrol car to pick her up and bring her to the hospital. You can call her from the car phone and let her know what is happening so she'll be ready for the car." Detective Hubert stated as he turned to leave the house.

Ron called his mother from the car phone while they were driving, the streets going by without Ron even being aware. He told his mother about Edith; about the call from the hospital and that a police car would be there to pick her up to bring her to the hospital where he would be waiting. He decided not tell her about what he had seen in the upstairs rooms of her older sister's house. He didn't yet know how to put all that into words.

For the remainder of the short ride, he sat in silence in the back seat, trying to make sense of this entire day. He wondered what was happening to his Aunt, but more importantly, what had already happened? He hoped she would be able to tell them something, but realized at the same time this was unlikely to happen. The hospital does not call the police to contact family if everything was fine. He knew this from the experience with his father, and that certainly had not turned out okay.

Once they had arrived at the hospital, the same nurse who had spoken to Ron earlier stopped them outside Edith's room.

"She's had another attack, the team is in with her now. You'll have to wait out here." She was very stern and would not answer any questions, either from the detectives or from Ron. The three had no choice but to wait until the doctor and her team came from the room.

"Mom." Ron jumped up as a woman slowly approached, followed slowly by a uniformed police officer. His mother shuffled forward and Ron hugged her small frame to him when they met. As usual, every grey hair was in place, but her face was lined with worry and fatigue. She looked older than she had just two days ago.

"The doctors are with her, mom, they said she's had another heart attack." Ron told her quietly.

The two walked slowly back to the uncomfortable chairs provided for hospital visitors. His mother was clearly uncomfortable. Something told Ron it was just because of the chairs. Ron made the introductions.

"Mrs. Walker, I realize this is a difficult time, but do you think you could answer a few questions for us?" Detective O'Leary asked gently after Mrs. Walker had sat down. Without really knowing why, Ron was glad she had been the one to ask questions of his mother.

"I don't know how I can help. I've been sick myself, you know, and haven't seen my sister for several weeks. Besides, why are the police involved with an old woman who had a heart attack?" she asked suspiciously, looking from the two detectives to her son.

Detective O'Leary leaned forward. "Mrs. Walker, we've been to your sisters' home. Actually, we just left there, with your son." She gestured toward Ron.

"We found some things that were . . . well, rather unexpected. I know Mr. Walker has told you about the marks on your sisters' back. That's what brought us here to start with, but after being to her home, we have quite a few questions that I hope you can help us with. Can you tell me if you sister was ever married and did she have children"?

The questions went unanswered for several minutes. Everyone waited patiently.

Ron looked at his mother, who looked back at him silently. He could not read her face, but then he had never been able to.

"Well," she said quietly, turning back to the detective. "Edith was married, but that was a very long time ago, as Ron knows, and I'm sure he's told you. Her husband walked out on her many years ago. Walked out and just never came back. I was married myself by the time he left. What is it that you found that you consider strange enough to hold the interest of two police officers who surely have more important work to do in this fair city of ours?" She looked directly at Detective O'Leary, her stare unblinking.

Ron continued looking at his mother and listening to her responses. She seemed to be very defensive, which was not like her at all. He knew from experience that she could be evasive when she wanted to be, but this was some how different.

"Mom," Ron interjected, glancing first at the detectives for the okay to go ahead, then back at her when they didn't object.

"At Aunt Edith's house, upstairs actually, we found a photograph. I saw it myself in her bedroom. In the photo are a man and two kids, but I don't know who they are. I also saw something else. There's a whip, laying on the floor in front of the picture."

Ron paused, not sure how much he really needed or wanted to share. When his mother made no comment, he continued.

"It looks like, well, it looks like she whipped her own back while sitting in front of that picture." Ron could see his mother was listening, but the blank look on her face concerned him. He looked to Detective O'Leary.

Silent Secrets

"Mrs. Walker, would you like a glass of water or something"? she asked gently.

June Walker shook her head, not even looking at the detectives.

"The doctor said her back is covered with scars and marks, mom. I saw the pictures they took of her back earlier today. There's blood on the whip, the mirror, the mat, everything. Nothing is making sense to me. Do you what's going on with her? Can you explain any of this?"

Ron looked at his mother. Wanting an answer, any answer, but hoping that she could provide one that would explain everything quickly. She looked back blankly at Ron, over at the two detectives, but said nothing.

Ron waited; the cops waited. Nothing. Just as Ron was ready to ask again, to insist on an answer, an explanation, believing she must know something that could help, the nurse intruded upon their circle and demanded everyone to follow her.

The four visitors moved slowly to the room Edith occupied, Ron walking slowly with his mother, knowing her legs hurt if she tried to walk to far or to fast. The detectives made their way in front. He realized she was not that old but at times she acted older than his Aunt.

When they arrived at his Aunt's room, Dr Main, who had attended her when she arrived, informed them that the emergency team had done everything they could for the woman.

"I'm very sorry, but there's nothing else we can do. She was very weak when she came in and this last attack was just too much for her. Please accept my condolences." Dr Main gently held June's hand as she spoke.

"A woman of this age, the damage to her heart is just to much. She also presents as malnourished, which also places a great strain on the heart, as you can well imagine. If she had seen a doctor on a regular basis," Dr Main explained, "things might have been different."

She was dead. The doctor continued talking, extending sympathies to the family, explaining more details, but Ron did not hear anything else. He reached out and held his mother's hand, neither knowing what to do or say at this moment.

The detectives moved away and spoke in whispers to the doctor father down the hall, leaving the last remaining family of a very lonely woman standing in the hospital hallway. Ron knew that his aunt never went to the doctor. She always said she didn't trust them, he doubted she had ever been to one in her life. The thought crossed his mind that he or his mother should have insisted, but what would have been the use?

Detective O'Leary had heard all that the doctor had said. Nothing suggested foul play. There were the marks on her back, which had brought them here to start with, but essentially, she had died of a combination of old age and a bad heart.

"Dr. Do you think it's possible that the marks on her back could be self inflicted?" Detective Hubert asked quietly

Silent Secrets

"Self inflicted? Why would someone do that?" the doctor responded. When neither detective offered an explanation, she continued. "I suppose, under certain circumstances, that could happen. What ever caused those marks certainly does not appear to be the cause of her death. I would say that a combination of poor eating habits and limited medical care combined decreased the life span of this woman. The autopsy, which I assume will occur, can certainly tell you more, but that is my opinion at this time." With that the doctor walked down the hall to speak with a nurse.

"Well, Bear, I think our job is done here, as they say. I don't see foul play, just a crazy old woman who maybe was into some self inflicted S&M. What's your take on the situation?" O'Leary glanced down the hall at mother and son.

Detective Hubert agreed. They could mark this one closed in his opinion. What people chose to do to themselves behind closed doors was not the business of the police.

Finally Detective O'Leary approached Ron and his mother.

"Mr. Walker, Mrs. Walker, the doctor says her heart just gave out. They will, of course, conduct an autopsy, which may reveal more. They said they tried everything. I'm so sorry for your loss. Detective Hubert and I are going to leave right now to let you two get things sorted out here. How can we get hold of you in the event that we need to?"

Both Ron and his mother gave the officer their home numbers and addresses, which she wrote down in the now familiar black book. Ron thought of his Aunt and her books.

Detective Hubert pulled Ron to one side before leaving.

"Listen, Mr. Walker. I um, that is, I, well, I just wanted to apologize for coming on to you so hard earlier. I don't like it when kids and old people get hurt. I see it a lot in this job. I, well . . . anyway, we're going to want to gather some items from your aunts' home, finish up a few things. Just basically make sure that is your aunts' blood. Not that I have any doubt mind you. Are you planning to go back there today?" Now it was the big detective who seemed uncomfortable. Ron found this rather humorous, even though he was not in a comical mood.

"No, I hadn't planned on going back. I mean I'm going to take my mother home. I think we need to talk, you know, try to figure out what's going on." Ron stated. He appreciated the apology from the big detective.

"Alright then, we'll contact you in a couple days, after the autopsy results are in. Maybe take another trip over to your aunts' house. If you do go there in the mean time, don't touch anything upstairs. Okay?"

Detective Hubert glanced over at Mrs. Walker. "Can you talk to your mother, try to find out about who those people might be? I'm sure she'll be able to help with that part at least. I think that might be important, even if no one besides your aunt caused those injuries. Do you have any other family that might be able to help? Cousins, aunts, grandparents?"

"No, there's just the three of us, oh, I guess I mean just the two of us, no one else. I'll ask mom about the picture, maybe she does know something." Ron turned back to look at his mother, who was still sitting with Detective O'Leary on the uncomfortable couch.

Ron went to his mother and reached for her hand.

"Come on, mom. Let's talk to the nurses and get the paper work done, then we can head home."

Ron smiled at Detective O'Leary as he reached down to help his mother up. Their eyes met for a brief second. This pleased Ron.

"I'll see you soon," she said. Ron hoped she was an honest person.

Chapter 5

Once they reached his mother's home, Ron kept himself busy by preparing a light supper for the two of them. The day had gone by quickly and he was starved. He watched her from the corner of his eye as he moved about the kitchen. He was trying to decide how to both ask for and get answers to, the hundreds of questions he now had about his aunt. She sat quietly at the small kitchen table, her favourite place in the whole house, Ron knew.

Seeing her sitting there, Ron was brought back to his child hood in this very house. His mother almost always where she was right now, when she wasn't at church. The house had a formal dining room but the family had rarely used it when they were together, preferring instead to eat in the kitchen, just the three of them every night.

This kitchen table was where she and his father had 'discussions' about what to do with Ron when he was going through his rebellious teen years. It's where the three played games or cards once a week on what his mother had called 'games night'. It's where Ron had done most of his homework, while his mother cleaned up the supper dishes, and his father busied himself with the paper. His parents' would be immediately available if he needed help with any of his problems. He hoped this was still the case because he really needed help today.

Silent Secrets

Ron looked around the room, realizing that little had changed in this room over the years. Oh, it had been painted many times and the appliances had been up dated over the years, but the feel of the room was the same. The uncluttered surfaces, so different from what he had seen this morning at Edith's, brought him comfort.

The kitchen remained the heart of the house, where all the important activities took place. He decided this was the best place to talk to his mother about today's events. Before he even began, he knew the conversation would be awkward after her silence at the hospital. She had just last her only sister but he still needed to know what was going on.

"Mom, are you okay?" he asked quietly as he brought the cup of tea he had made for her to the table and sat down across from her. He reached out for her hand, folding it in his own larger hand, something she had done for him when he had been younger and upset. That had been when his hand had still fit inside hers. That seemed to be a long time ago now.

She looked across the table at him as if she had just been woken from a daydream by the touch of his hand. She smiled briefly, but to Ron, her eyes appeared to be seeing something far away.

"Yes, Ron, I'm okay. It's just that . . . well; it's just us now. Just the two of us." She took a sip of her tea, setting the cup down carefully on the saucer, being careful not to spill the hot liquid.

"Mom, I don't understand any of this. So much has happened in such a short time. I really need your help to make sense of this. Why do you think Aunt Edith would whip herself like that?"

His mother remained silent for several minutes, looking at him, but not really seeing him as he waited patiently for an answer.

"I don't know, Ron. Sometimes, like I said earlier, I think we don't really know much about any one, especially the people we think we know best. I guess we'll never really know what she was thinking or why she lived the way she did. She was all alone in that big house, never even going to church," his mother said.

Still not looking at him, she said, quietly, "Sometimes, I think it's better not to know too much."

"But mom, who are the people be in the picture I told you about? Have you ever seen that picture, ever been upstairs or in her room?" Ron had so many questions; he wasn't sure where to start.

When she didn't answer, he continued. "There was a man, and two little children. It was a black and white photo so it looks like it was taken a long time ago. Who are they? Why would she have their picture set up like that? Why would she hurt herself in front of them, in front of a mirror for that matter? Come on mom, help me here," Ron pleaded.

He paused, not really sure what to say or how to ask what he needed to know. She remained silent, not looking at him at all.

"I really need to understand all this," Ron said as he stood up to return to the stove where he was heating some tomato soup for his mother and himself. He was trying to keep himself busy with the stirring of the soup, hoping this would help his mother relax enough to answer his questions. From behind him, he heard her finally speak.

"We need to call the funeral home, Ron, to make the final arrangements for Edith. I think you should do that, being the man of the house. I know she wanted to be cremated; she always said that. Never wanted to 'take up space better left to the living', is what she always said. Who do we call, Ron? How long, do you think, until they finish the autopsy?"

From her tone, Ron knew any further inquiries about his aunt's life were not going to be answered right now. He knew from experience that when his mother did not want to talk about something, she just ignored everyone and went on with something else, as if nothing had been asked of her. He remembered how frustrated his father would get with this behaviour, how it had frustrated him when they had lived together. Ron knew better than to push any further right now. Any more questions would have to wait for another day.

"I'll make the arrangements," Ron said as he turned the soup to low before leaving the room to make the inquiries from the living room phone. This task at least was something he understood how to do.

When he returned to the kitchen, his mother still sat where he had left her, but now he saw she had a long envelope in her hand, turning it over and over absently.

"This is for you, Ron. Edith gave me this to hold for you many years ago. She told me I was to give it to you when she died." His mother passed him the envelope, not looking at him as she did so. She picked up her cup and took a drink of the now cooling tea. Ron could see a slight shaking in her hand, which she tried to contain by using two hands on the little cup.

Ron was puzzled. In his hand was a letter from a woman who had just died. His stomach felt like a beehive. He saw his name scrawled on the front of the envelope in his aunts' distinct penmanship. He would recognize that handwriting anywhere. He tore open the end of the yellowed envelope. Inside was a single sheet of folded lined paper.

He quietly read the short note aloud to his mother.

"This letter is intended for the only person important to me in my life. I leave all my worldly possessions, including my home, to Ronald Walker. I hope you find the peace and happiness you deserve there," Ron read.

His aunt had signed the note in her familiar loopy signature, and someone else had signed the note beside her as her witness. It was dated just over ten years ago. At the bottom of the note, below the signatures, was another notation that had been added by Edith. Ron read this out as well.

"The burden of life can be heavy, but we must each bear it as best we can."

He stood silently with the note in his hand for several minutes, not sure what, if anything, to say. He had hoped for answers, but the letter gave him nothing but more questions and confusion.

"I don't understand, mom." He finally said. "She left every thing to me? Why mom? Why not to you, her only sister?" Ron asked as he put the note on the table and sank into the chair across from his mother.

June looked up from her teacup and smiled. "I'm sure she thought you could use it far more than me, dear. I have everything I need right here. The last thing I need is to be burdened, at my age, with her old house and all the junk it contains." She glanced at the stove.

"I'm sure that soup is long ready, Ron. Let's have some supper. It's been a trying day for both of us." For some reason, Ron thought she sounded relieved. Why that would be he did not know.

Again the dismissive tone was evident in her voice. Ron knew the subject was closed. They ate in silence at the kitchen table, each lost in their own thoughts, or at least Ron knew he was. More than just lost, drowning, in fact.

When they were done eating, Ron's mother stood.

"Just leave the dishes on the table, Ron. I've had a long day, so I'm going up to have a hot soak and read for a while to relax my weary bones. Why don't you head home? There's nothing else to be done for today." She kissed Ron and walked slowly toward the back of the house, to the bedroom she had shared for many years with his father.

"Don't forget to lock up in case I fall asleep. Call me tomorrow, dear." With that she was gone, leaving Ron alone at the table, with only his letter for company.

Ron left the house, locking the door behind him and headed back to his own home, still without any answers to his many questions and even more questions than he had started with this morning. He lived less then 8 blocks away from his mothers' home and in no time was at his own apartment without any recollection of the passage of time. Fortunately, with his head once again clearly in the clouds, he had not been run down on the street or accosted by strangers.

He glanced at his watch as he unlocked the scarred door of his apartment. Nearly 7 PM. He had been gone since early this morning. Not a long time really, he thought, and yet in that short time so many things had changed. He fell on the worn couch, exhausted and mentally drained from the strain of the day. As he fell asleep, he visualized the scarred back of his aunt once again.

He awoke to the sound of his phone ringing insistently, as only a phone can do when you are asleep. He could see the light had shifted, but he had no idea what time it was. Without getting up, he reached over and picked up the instrument from the table in front of the couch on which he lay.

Not surprisingly, it was the pastor from his mother's church, calling to extend the sympathies of the congregation and offering services if Ron required them. Ron listened to him, trying to respond in a non-committal fashion at the right times.

Silent Secrets

It was a difficult conversation for Ron. He had not been to church in many years, but still knew the pastor. When Ron had decided to stop going to church in his early teens, his mother had been very upset. The church was very important to her and she wanted it to be that way for Ron. She had invited the pastor over for dinner one night to have him try to convince Ron to return to the flock.

Finally his father had intervened, bless his heart, telling his mother and the pastor to leave the boy alone. His father insisted Ron was old enough now to make up his own mind. His father then went on to tell them both that a boy didn't have to attend church to be a good person.

Ron had loved the man at that moment, and knew that what his father said was true. His father had never been inside a church in his entire life, except for the day of his wedding, and yet the world could not ask for a kinder or more caring man. From that day on, Ron had never returned to the church and never again felt that he needed to. Like his father, he held his own religion and felt that was enough. His mother, of course, continued to attend regularly. She thankfully respected him in his decision, with the support of his father, and did not push him any further.

After finally hanging up with the pastor, Ron glanced at his watch. 8:30 on Sunday morning. Now he understood why the pastor had called him. His mother would already be at the church, having gone for the early sermon as she usually did, then probably staying to help out with one of the other activities. A typical Sunday for her would include the whole day spent at the church, especially since his dad had died.

After starting the coffee maker in the small kitchen, Ron sat on his couch, thinking, while his morning coffee slowly perked. The sun streamed in through the curtain less window. The day promised to be one of reflection, Ron realized.

His father, cut down in the prime of his life. Hit by a drunk driver who had never even bothered to stop. The same man who, when finally found by the authorities, was duly punished by the great legal system with 2 years less a day to be served at the local summer camp, as the jail was commonly referred to. Two years, minus one day, was apparently the going rate for a man that could not be replaced. The courts, in their wisdom, had decided the driver had been to drunk to be held fully responsible; after all, he was an upstanding businessman with no previous record. He had not planned on killing anyone. The loss of his father, the waste of such a wonderful man, had been a hard blow to Ron, who to this day missed the wise words of the eloquent and wise man that had been his father. Even after all this time, the entire incident made him very angry.

He wished again desperately his father were here to help figure this situation out. His common sense had kept Ron grounded all his life.

Ron tried to think of the last time his father had seen his Aunt, but could not. Ron could not recall his father ever going with them for their Saturday visits. He knew his dad would go over to her house on occasion to fix things, like when the pipe burst in the bathroom or when the furnace wouldn't kick in one year. Ron had gone with him to help but his father had never stayed long, never really spoke to Edith. Together they just did the job that had been asked of him by his wife and left. Helping out was what his mother expected them to do for her sister and so it was done. Even as a child, Ron knew it had been an unusual relationship. His father had never complained as far as Ron knew and yet Ron always felt that his father had resented that he was expected to be the man of both households. Now Ron could appreciate this himself.

The more he thought of it, the more Ron realized his father had never spoken either to or about Edith, at least not when Ron had been around. Ron really had no idea what he had thought of her. Another question that would remain unanswered.

Ron recalled many positive and supportive times with his father, like when he had jumped to his defense when Ron did not want to come home from teachers' college to spend his weekends with his Aunt. He wanted to spend what free time he had with his friends and his father had agreed.

His father had said to his mother, "Let things be, June, what's done is done, it's time to let the past go. He's a grown man and needs to make his own way in this world. We've given him all we can."

Ron never forgot these words, said in one of the few arguments his parents ever had. He also never really understood what his dad meant by these comments, but clearly his mother had understood. Surprisingly, from then on, his mother had dropped the subject, at least when his father was around.

After his father's death, Ron did eventually return to visit his Aunt, but this was his own choice. He never really understood why. Maybe because he knew it was so important to both his mother and his Aunt. They were, after all, all the family he had left. Maybe he missed the routine? He didn't know then and really didn't know now.

As he sat smelling the aromatic smell of the coffee coming from the kitchen he thought about his aunt. She never did anything to hurt him or purposely scare him. In fact, she was always very kind to him. She taught him, in the silence of her beloved garden, to appreciate the plants, flowers and food that she grew there. She taught him to look at a bug as something that was good for the world, not something just to be killed, as he had wanted to do as a small child when he came upon them suddenly.

He smiled as he recalled one time when he was young and she had shown him how to capture a caterpillar in the fall. They had placed it in a jar with the proper leaves for food and a branch on which it could cocoon. She then told him to wait while it grew into a butterfly. Every Saturday he would run to the jar to see if the caterpillar had emerged into a butterfly. He remembered this event fondly. It still made him smile to recall how the butterfly had opened during one of his Saturday visits with his mother. He had been mystified and elated, watching the butterfly break out of the cocoon, it's wings folded close to its body but slowly opening. He watched mesmerized while it dried its wings and tried to fly inside the now to small bottle.

Ron had wanted to keep the butterfly contained in that jar so he could take it home. Edith had told him all creatures needed to be free, so he and Edith had let it go in the garden before he left. It had flown from the jar, up and away. Ron quickly lost sight of the orange and black wings in the bright sunlight.

Ron was interrupted in his travels down memory lane by the sound of knocking on his door. Who would be visiting him at this hour, it wasn't even noon and Ron rarely had company in his small apartment. He hoped it wasn't the pastor, sent by his mother to bring him back to the flock in his hour of need.

As he approached the door, he could hear the irritating noise of a small dog yapping. As soon as he heard this, he knew it was the building superintendent, not the pastor. Now, he thought, he would prefer it to be the pastor. The superintendent always traveled with his dog, the yappy one that ran around like a rat just let out of his cage. Ron opened his door slightly, just enough to peer out. He didn't want the rat to run in or the superintendent would be sure to follow, just like Mary and her lambs.

"Hey man, how're things going for you? Just stopped by to let you know your water's gonna get turned off from Monday morning while we're workin' on the plumbing. Mrs. C, you know, on the third floor, had a leak so we need to shut everything off to fix the problem." The man at the door informed Ron.

Ron kept an eye on the rat as the superintendent spoke. It was running around, clearly trying to catch some imaginary ghost in the hall.

Finally Ron looked away from the scurrying ball of fur in the hall and returned his attention to his unwanted visitor.

"How long will the water be off this time, Larry? And while you're here, I'm just curious. What are the chances that we're going to have heat this coming winter?"

Ron had never liked the superintendent. He was sure that, two years ago when Larry took over the job, he had some how rigged the furnace so all the heat in the building went to his apartment and none to the other tenants' units. Ron wasn't sure how he had done it, but something was definitely wrong. For the first two years Ron had lived here before Larry was superintendent, the heat had been fine.

Old Mr. Hake had been very good at making sure that every one was comfortable and anything that needed to be fixed was done right away, if at all possible. Before becoming superintendent, Larry had been a tenant like Ron. Then he was always grouching about the heat, complaining about the cold, even though it had been fine as far as Ron remembered. Now, Larry never complained about the heat, in fact, some winter days you could see his windows open, the curtains blowing in the wind, while the tenants on the upper floors layered themselves in sweaters.

"Hey man," Larry said, "I've been lookin' at that old monster all summer and can't find a single thing wrong. You let me know if there's any problem when it gets cold outside and I'll get right on it. You can count on that." Larry promised, probably sounding to the inexperienced like he might actually mean it.

"Yeah, right." Ron imagined Larry would just jump right up in the middle of the night to get the heat working for everyone else in the building.

"How long is the water going to be off? And why do you need to turn off every ones water? I thought you said the leak was upstairs?" Ron wasn't really interested in the answer, but he was curious about what Larry was up to now.

"Well I can't say for how long exactly, maybe an hour, maybe the whole day. I'm gonna upgrade some of the pipes when I fix the leak, so I need all the water off. Anyway, you have a nice day. I gotta go make sure every one knows about the water."

Larry smiled his greasy, yellow-toothed smile, picked up the still running rat and shuffled down the hall. The rat kept yapping back over his shoulder while Larry carried it down the hall to the next apartment.

Ron didn't know the couple that lived next door, they had just moved in last month with their small baby. He could imagine their reaction when they heard they would be without water for the whole day. They'd get used to such occurrences, Ron was sure.

Ron could believe that Larry was 'upgrading' the water pipes, which more than likely meant Larry was somehow going to benefit, while the rest of the building lost out. Ron was at a loss to figure out how, but there was sure to be some benefit to Larry that the other tenants would never know about.

Ron had lived in this apartment for four years, having taken it because it was both cheap and close to work, which meant that he could walk, even on bad weather days. When he had first been offered the position at the school on the next block, Ron had been happy to find the apartment. Now he was tired of it. Four years at the same school was a good thing, Ron thought, but four years in this place was a different story all together.

Granted, the cheap rent had allowed him to save up some money. Those wonderful vacations, to the sun and sand while every one else was shoveling snow, had certainly made living in the bleak apartment more bearable.

Things have certainly changed now, Ron thought. He had certainly never expected that Edith would give her house to him. But do I want it? He asked himself. It was a very big house for one person. Mind you, Edith had lived there all alone for years and she seemed to have managed okay.

Thinking of what happened in the house, what had been going on upstairs, he wasn't sure he would be able to erase the memory of her room from his head. Maybe he could sell it, buy something else, or maybe just rent it out to someone else for now. Well, all that could be sorted out later, Ron thought. Today I need to get organized.

Ron first contacted his principal at home to ask for a couple days leave due to a family death. He then contacted the funeral home to ask if the body had been released from the morgue yet. He was told that Edith was expected to arrive the following day and would then be available to be cremated on Tuesday. Ron and his mother had agreed there would be no service, no display of the body. It was not something that his aunt would have wanted, nor did Ron or his mother expect anyone to show up. As Mr. Wells had stated, her only visitor, besides Ron and his mom, had been his wife, a woman long dead; it was unlikely she would show up at a funeral parlour or hang around to listen to a eulogy.

This thought made Ron smile briefly. If Mrs. Wells did show up, he wondered what the funeral director would do with a ghost floating around the visiting room. When he realized he was smiling, he stopped. He suddenly felt guilty for thinking like this. His aunt had just died; he some how didn't think it was right to smile at a time like this.

He needed to clear his head and think for a while. Ron decided he would take a walk. The day was again cool and yet the sun outside made him feel good. It was like the last hurrah for the summer. Ron was determined not to waste it holed up in an apartment he would likely be stuck in for the next few months while winter blew around outside, and sometimes inside through the old windows, unless he moved of course.

Ron always enjoyed his time walking the neighbourhood or sitting at the park. He watched the people who spent their time there. He would often see a lot of mothers and fathers with their young children in tow, playing on the swings or tossing a ball around. Sometimes he ran into one of his students. This let him get to know them a little bit outside the sterile environment of the classroom. Today as he sat on the bench below a large oak tree now nearly devoid of leaves, he recognized one of his students, Bill Whittaker, racing by on his bike.

"Hey Mr. Walker, how're you doing?" the boy called out, before coming to a stop and returning with his bike to the bench where Ron sat.

"Hey, Bill, how are you? Great day for a bike ride."

"Yeah it's great. We're gonna shoot a few hoops. Do you wanna play pick up with us? We got a game going over behind the fountain?" Bill asked, gesturing behind him towards the blacktop area where old basketball hoops had been installed years ago. Ron had used this same area with his own friends as a child.

Ron was about to decline the invitation when he decided this might be exactly what he needed. He liked basketball and besides, it's not like he had a lot of other things to do right now. He hoped the physical activity and interaction might be just what he needed.

Ron spent a couple of hours playing with a dozen kids, about half from his school and the others, some past school age, from the surrounding neighbourhood. Every one had a great time and the adrenalin helped Ron clear his head. Following the game, he headed home, sweaty, but mentally relaxed for the first time in what seemed like a like time.

By the time he was back at his apartment, he thought he knew what he had to do now, at least what he wanted to do. First he called the two detectives, but was told neither was in. He left a message asking one of them to call him back, stating just that he had a few questions for one of them.

He filled the rest of the day with house keeping jobs; the ones that he usually completed on Saturdays but had obviously not had the time to do. As Ron was finishing up his supper dishes, the few, that is, which he had made with his great supper of leftovers, his phone rang.

"Mr. Walker, it's Detective O'Leary, returning your call." Her voice was as he remembered and for a minute Ron forgot why he had called in the first place. Her face floated in the air in front of him as if she were actually in the room.

"Oh, yes, um, detective, well," Ron stuttered. "I was calling about my aunt. Ah, what I mean is, about her house. Well, what I mean to say is, she left her house to me." Ron stammered into the phone, the usual easy flow of words he used in the classroom gone from his head. He mentally hit himself in the forehead, hoping to jar his brain into use.

"Mr. Walker, I'm not sure I understand. Is there something you need, or something I can help you with? Have you found something at her house I should know about?" Detective O'Leary asked.

Ron thought it sounded like she was smiling. With him or at him, he wondered briefly.

He couldn't help but think that there was a kindness towards him in her voice, as if she really did want to help him. But maybe that was just his wishful thinking. Either way, it gave him the confidence to continue his conversation. He was glad it was her and not her partner that had returned his call.

"What I need to know is, can I move into my aunts house or do the police need something else there?" He asked. No stammer now, he was glad to hear.

"Well actually, we've just received the results of the autopsy and there is no indication of foul play, as we guessed after seeing her room. So, as far as I know, the police will have nothing further to do with your aunts' death. Are you thinking of moving into her house soon?" Detective O'Leary asked.

"Well, my mom gave me this letter yesterday, after we left the hospital. It was from my aunt. In it she said she left her house to me. This place I live in, well, it's not great and I've been thinking all day . . ." Ron stopped in mid sentence, not sure what he should say or even why he was telling her this. He felt he was babbling again and imagined her on the other end of the line, rolling her eyes to the ceiling, hoping he would just say goodbye.

"Does this sound morbid to you?" He finally asked. Suddenly it was important to know what she thought. Ron had no idea why, but it was very important to him at this moment.

"Mr. Walker, I would like to look at your aunt's place one more time, just to be sure we didn't missed anything on our last visit, since it was cut a bit short. Not that I'm expecting to find anything. Of course, that's if you don't object. Like I said, at this time your aunt's death doesn't appear to be a police matter. If you're going to be moving in, perhaps my partner and I could come by. Say Monday or Tuesday? Just to have another look around with you. If you can let me know what time you expect to be home from work, we can arrange it then. Would that be okay? And no, I don't think it is morbid, I think you must have been very close to your aunt." Again the voice was both sympathetic and genuine.

"Actually I've taken a couple days off work, so I think I'll go over to the house tomorrow morning and try to get things straight in my head. You're welcome to come by whenever you want." Ron had purposely not included her partner in the invitation. Ron very much wanted her to come by alone. He knew it was unlikely that she would, she was after all, involved with his as part of her job.

This surprised him, this sudden intense feeling toward her. He was usually rather reserved around women, taking a long time to build up enough courage to ask for a date, but he knew this was where he was headed. He wondered if this was just a reaction to the sudden death of his aunt, but just as quickly dismissed the idea. He liked Detective O'Leary, of that he was certain.

"Okay, Mr. Walker. I'll let Detective Hubert know when he returns. We'll try to swing by tomorrow sometime. Even though everything looks pretty straight forward, can I ask you not to disturb anything in the bedroom upstairs until we arrive?"

"To be honest, I'm not sure I'll even be able to go in that room right now. It's not something I really want to see again or for that matter, even think about. But I guess I don't have much choice there. I'll be there tomorrow and I'll be here at my place tonight if you need to get hold of me. Thank you, Detective O'Leary".

Ron hung up the phone, still thinking about the room and the detective, as if they were somehow intertwined. He wasn't sure why he had told her he would be home tonight. What exactly had he expected her to say to that?

Cindy LaChance

Back at the station house, Sandy O'Leary was having her own struggle with the conversation. When Bear arrived, she pulled him aside to have a conversation she did not want over heard. She explained about the call from Ron Walker and what she had said to him in response.

"You know as well as I do, Jr., that we have nothing at that house to investigate. I'm guessing you want to go there for another reason?" Bear was a very perceptive man and Sandy respected his opinions.

"Well, I know we were looking at him as a suspect but that clearly is not the case now. I just like the guy. Any reason I shouldn't go?" She asked, hoping he would not find one.

"Nope, no reason at all. You enjoy your time off however you want." Her old friend put his hand on her shoulder and squeezed gently. "We all need down time in a job like this and I know you don't take much."

Sandy smiled in return, knowing he was right. She did little else away from the job and besides; she had liked this Ron guy from the minute they met. She was very happy the way everything turned out, except of course the death of the old lady, but that was beyond her control.

By 9 AM Monday morning, Ron was back at his aunt's house. The morning had brought the sun, again strong and bright, streaming in through the living room windows that had been freed, for the first time in years, of their heavy drapes. This was the first thing Ron had done when he arrived there. He had gone around and pulled back all the other curtains on the main floor, letting the sun flow through the usually dark interior.

How different everything looked in the natural light of day, he thought, as he looked around with new eyes. The space was not just his aunts' house any longer; the house was now his to do with as he wanted. He knew there was a lot to do. Already plans were formulating in his head.

He thought briefly of his last girlfriend. She had complained non-stop about his apartment, trying to get him to move to a nicer place, but he had resisted. Wouldn't she be surprised to find out he now owned a place of his own? The thought made him smile in the empty room. Well, she was long gone. The future did not include her.

The shadows had fallen away from the corners of the rooms as the curtains had been pulled back, showing off the cluttered contents of each room as well as the layers of dust that covered every surface. Ron had always been aware of the clutter, but now the exact nature of the clutter could be seen more clearly.

The living room, heavy with books on every shelf and surface, also had boxes piled on top of each other on the floor, junk mail piled on top of these. Ron shook his head in wonder as he looked around; it seemed like his aunt had kept every piece of paper she had ever received. He had no idea why she had been such a pack rat with all this useless garbage.

His parents had been the exact opposite, keeping only what they needed and what they used. His father, in particular, had always been the one to constantly purge the home, not wanting it to become a 'museum of natural history', as he used to say. Ron definitely took after his parents and not his aunt in that respect.

He walked slowly through the now brighter, but still cluttered kitchen, and out the back door to the rear garden that his aunt had prized so much. Here the clutter ended. The small wooden deck held two chairs, one to each side of the door. He had spent many hours sitting in these chairs with his aunt. The two of them just listening to the sounds of the garden; the birds flying over head, calling each other with their never ending message, the bees buzzing around the flowers, pollinating them, and the sounds of the occasional vehicle from the street melding with these sounds. Occasionally Ron, but never by Edith, would break this quiet.

When he was younger, he would spend his time on this deck drawing the garden flowers or the birds sitting in the trees. He had thought he was pretty good then, his aunt had given him the paper and had always smiled and nodded at his creations.

As he matured, he realized this was not a talent area for him. If nothing else, the works of art seemed to give his aunt some satisfaction. He had seen most of this poor artwork stacked on the bookshelf in the living room, along with the small box of shells and pebbles she had let him play with as a child.

The garden itself was fairly empty now, he saw. The vegetables had been picked a couple months before, eaten or canned for the winter as usual. The pear trees were dropping their leaves on the browning grass beneath, the fruit long since picked and preserved as well. His aunt didn't waste anything the garden offered her. Ron recalled many days as a child climbing those old trees, collecting the fruit from the upper branches before they fell to the ground or just sitting up there watching the world move around him, but from a higher perspective.

He noticed now that the trees needed pruning and decided this was something he should do before the real cold set in. This had been his job for several years, his aunt pointing out the branches to be cut and Ron doing the actual work. This year, he would be on his own for that job, he thought sadly.

His silent reverie was disturbed by the sound of knocking from the front door, bringing him back to the present. As he arrived at the front hall he could see through the open front door, a woman standing on the porch, waiting patiently for him.

For a second he had hoped it was Detective O'Leary, minus her partner, but realized quickly his mistake and was immediately disappointed. The woman held a clipboard in one hand and a small black purse clutched in the other. A friend of his aunt's he wondered or a salesperson more likely, no doubt coming by to sell some useless item no one would buy from a store.

"Yes? Can I help you?" He asked as he opened the door further, ready to close it if the saleswoman became too pushy.

"Oh, excuse me, sir. I'm here to see Mrs. McKellridge," she said, her crisp British accent lilting in the air.

Ron was taken aback for a moment. He hadn't really expected the woman to know his aunts name.

"I'm sorry, my aunt, well, she's just passed away. Is there something I can do for you?" He asked cautiously.

"Oh dear, I'm so sorry, sir. Please accept my condolences. What a terrible tragedy. I didn't know." She stammered, and then appeared to regain her composure.

"This is rather awkward for me, coming at a time like this. I'm from the Mission. As I'm sure you know, Mrs. McKellridge always donated boxes of canned goods for our Christmas celebrations. People loved them you know. I came by to see if she was going to this year . . . but," she trailed off, clearly not knowing what to say next.

Donated her canned goods, was all Ron heard.

"She gave away her food? All the things we canned? How much did she give away to your Mission? How long has she been doing this?" Ron was perplexed, but stopped himself so the woman could answer.

So many more questions popped into his head, more questions and fewer answers. Once again, more things to add to the ever growing list of things that he didn't know about his aunt.

"Well, I'm not sure how long she has been involved with us. I've been with the Mission for ten years now, you know, volunteering my time for the less fortunate of this city, like Mrs. McKellridge did so generously. She's given food every year that I've been involved. Usually I come by to set a time for the pick up, and then a couple of men come by to actually pick everything up.

Usually I just phone people but . . ." She stopped, looking at her clipboard. "I'm sorry, this must be a very bad time for you. Please, again, accept my condolences." She stood awkwardly on the step.

"No, no. I'm sorry. All this is just so new to me; there is just so much I need to learn about my aunt. I'm not really sure what to do. I'll look around and see what she had ready for your program, okay? I'll call you next week, okay" What else was he supposed to say?

She agreed this would be a good plan. She handed Ron a business card with the Mission phone number and address on it. He told her he would call if he found anything his aunt had decided to donate, that way she would not have to return for no reason.

Ron was about to close the door when a car pulled up in front. Detective O'Leary exited from the driver's side, alone.

"Hey, nice to see you again" Ron beamed. I have to stop acting like an imbecile, he thought to himself. She's here on business, not to see you, you idiot.

The detective walked up the steps, also smiling.

"My partner is off today, but I thought I would come by anyway. I hope I haven't come at a bad time," she said, glancing at the woman who had just left the stoop to get into her own car parked by the curb.

"No, no, it's fine. She's from some homeless charity or something; she came by to collect a donation my aunt apparently gave every year. I didn't know anything about it." He paused, holding up the card and shaking his head.

"I guess there's a lot I didn't know anything about. 'Live and Learn' I guess. Rather I want to or not. Please, come on in. I was just out back in the garden. I've opened up all the curtains down here. It helps a bit." Ron felt like he was bumbling again, but couldn't help himself. He knew he needed to get himself under control.

"Mr. Walker . . ."

"Please, call me Ron. Only bill collectors or my students call me Mr. Walker." He smiled at his weak joke and was happy to see that she did also.

"Okay, Ron. Look, we've discussed the case, like I told you on the phone. We've also had a chance to look at the hospital and autopsy reports. There really is no indication of any foul play here. So, like I said, there's no need for the police to be involved at all." Ron followed her as she made her way to the living room, where she glanced around quickly as she spoke to him.

"Wow, there's more stuff here then I remember. I guess your aunt liked to read, eh?" she asked.

"Oh yes, she certainly loved to read. I always gave her books at Christmas and for her birthday. I knew that was a safe gift that she would like and use. It looks like she kept every single one I gave her, along with every newspaper or magazine we ordered for her as well. Coming here every week, I knew the house was crowded, but

I never realized just how much of a pack rat she was, or maybe I just didn't pay attention. Then there is the upstairs . . ." Ron trailed off for a minute, lost in his own thoughts.

"I'm glad to hear that the police don't think someone hurt my aunt. I just can't imagine that. But I also can't imagine anyone wanting to hurt them selves like that either. That doesn't make any sense to me at all. My aunt was just a harmless old lady," Ron tried to explain; although he didn't know why he felt he had to explain any thing.

They sat in silence for a bit, each looking around the room in the bright sunlight.

"Ron, did you get a chance to talk to your mom about any of this? Can she shed any light on what was found upstairs?" Detective O'Leary finally asked.

"My mom. Well, that's another story. When she doesn't want to talk about something, she just changes the subject. I learned a long time ago to let things be if it happens, so when I asked about Aunt Edith and the picture, she did just that. I didn't learn a thing, except that the house is now mine. That information came from the letter though, not from Mom. Who knows, maybe she doesn't know anything either. She's quite a few years younger than Edith, but I don't know much about their early years. Another subject that always got side tracked." Ron was rambling again and he knew it.

"Look, can I ask a favour while you're here, Detective O'Leary?" he leaned forward in his chair, looking at her, not sure how to ask the question that was on his mind.

"Sure, ask away Ron. But please, since we're being less formal, and I don't have to consider you a suspect any longer, call me Sandy."

"Sandy?"

"Well, that's my name"

"Oh, right, of course, sorry, I'm a bit scattered today. You considered me a suspect?" This took Ron by surprise.

"Well, really just a 'person of interest' as we say, and only initially until we figured this out. You understand, don't you?" Sandy smiled at him.

"Of course. Sorry. I never really thought about things that way. And certainly not with me involved. But I watch the cop shows on T.V." He paused for a second to gather his thoughts. "Any way, Sandy, would you come back upstairs with me, take another look at my aunts' room? I know I have to clean that stuff up, but . . . well, it would help if someone else were there with me. It's a bit weird up there." Ron asked.

"Sure, I understand. It's not something you expect to have to deal with every day. Do you have any garbage bags? We could gather everything up and put it in a bag. At least that way it would be out of sight." Sandy suggested, as she stood ready to go.

After Ron found garbage bags amidst the items packed under the kitchen sink, the two carefully ascended the still cluttered stairs together.

Silent Secrets

"You know, before the other day when you asked me to join you up here, I'd never been upstairs in this house. Strange, eh? When I was little, my mom made me stay with her, usually in the living room or kitchen unless we were outside in the garden. As I got older, there never seemed any reason to come upstairs. I always sat with Aunt Edith in the living room, or we worked in the kitchen or garden. I never really thought about the rest of the house, you know. I just stayed down stairs or in the garden. But now, well, it seems funny to have visited this house for all those years and never come upstairs." Ron seemed to be trying to explain, he just wasn't sure to who. Sandy said nothing.

They had arrived at the master bedroom door and Ron instinctively stopped. Slowly he reached out to open the closed door. He wasn't sure why he was so nervous, he already knew what he was going to find. Finally he pushed the door open, turning on the light as he did so. Everything was, of course, as they had left it. The room still perfectly made up, the corner of the bed still slightly rumpled from where Ron had sat during his first visit, the strange alter off to one side. Ron went first and opened the curtains. He couldn't help himself, the new and intruding light created even stranger shadows.

"I can't stand these curtains closed. I don't even have curtains at my place, except in the bedroom. I love the sun, I guess. I want to see it shining as often as I can. Somehow sunlight also makes all this more, I don't know, real, I guess." He waved his hand from side to side.

"Although, right now, I wish it weren't real," he said almost to himself. He had not yet moved away from the sunny window.

He noticed Sandy had already moved to the mirror, being careful not to step on the mat, which lay on the floor. She cautiously picked up the picture, examining it carefully, turning it over to inspect the back as well, as Ron had done with the Polaroid at the hospital. The plain wooden frame provided no clues as to who the people might be. The flat, black paper back was also blank. It could have come from anywhere. Briefly it flashed through her mind that the people could be models, their picture in the frame from when it was purchased. She had heard of that somewhere, people leaving those photos in, but no, it didn't seem like the right answer in this situation. These were real people, somehow connected to Edith.

"There's nothing written on the outside here. Sometimes people write on the back of the actual picture, you know, so years later they'll be able to remember who is in a picture or when it was taken. The people look real enough, like a real family I mean, not some picture from a magazine or something. If you like, we could take it out of the frame, see if anything is written on the back of the picture itself, under the backing?" Sandy suggested as she stood holding the photo.

Ron nodded in agreement at the suggestion and Sandy quickly opened the back to slide the picture out. The picture itself, having been protected by the glass, was untainted by the spattered blood. As Sandy turned it over, Ron automatically stepped closer to look as well. In his aunts' large, unique writing he read out loud what was written there.

It simply said "Good Bye" in thick, heavy black ink. It looked like something else might have been written there as well, but it was smudged so much that neither Sandy nor Ron could make it out. They looked at each other, then back at the words, trying to figure out what this one word could possibly mean.

"I didn't know your aunt, so, your best guess Ron. Does that look like her writing to you?" Sandy asked as she held up the photo.

"Definitely. She had very strange writing for an adult, big and loopy, almost like a kid when they're first learning to write cursive." Ron paused. "Now I'm even more confused. I really need to find out who these people are, or more likely, were. They must mean something to Aunt Edith." He straightened up and glanced at the window again. "My mother must know something about this," he said quietly to the sun.

"I'll put the picture here on the dresser and we can clean up the other stuff." Sandy stated as she walked over to the dresser. "I think the picture is the most important item right now."

After rolling up the mat, she put it, along with the whip, in the garbage bag they had brought upstairs. Ron tied this closed and put it out of view in the closet where his aunts' clothing hung neatly. Together they returned to the hall.

"We didn't go in the other rooms when we were last here. Have you looked in those other rooms yet, Ron"?

"No, but maybe I should while you're still here. Just in case we find something I would have to explain to the police." Ron laughed nervously. "Does that sound strange to you?"

"No, not strange, given the circumstances. Don't worry about it. This whole situation would be creepy for any one. Let's take a look now before I go." Sandy stated as she moved towards the first door.

They opened this door to find a bathroom. It looked like any bathroom you might find in any house, but not in this house. Unlike the bathroom on the first floor that Ron had been in many times, this one was clean and well organized. There was no clutter, no collection of used towels hanging over the rod, no variety of lotions on the counter like in the bathroom downstairs. It was a four-piece bath, painted in a light yellow colour with matching curtains and towels hanging from the rod beside the sparkling clean tub. The painted walls did not look freshly painted, but they were clean. On the sink sat a glass with four toothbrushes, two big and two small ones, each a different colour. They looked like they had never been used. On the edge of the tub sat two small rubber ducks, the kind children play with in the tub. They looked unused as well. Ron and Sandy looked at each other in what was becoming a familiar perplexed exchange.

"Okay, your aunt didn't have any children, we know that. But could someone else have been living here with her, boarders maybe living here upstairs? Someone with children?" Sandy asked. It seemed a logical explanation for what they were looking at.

"Someone else? What do you mean? I mean, no, no one else ever lived here, I'm sure of that. I've never seen anyone here. You think she had people hiding up here when I came to visit? Surely if kids lived here, Mr. Wells would have mentioned seeing them at sometime."

Ron backed away from the bathroom door, back into the hallway, breathing hard, his mind a whirlwind, a repeat of his reaction upon first entering his aunts' bedroom yesterday. At least there was no blood in this room. For that he was thankful.

"Well, I meant more like maybe she took in boarders or something, you know, to help with the bills. Maybe even some one involved with that Mission she gave food to? Did you say your aunt worked? This is a big house to keep up with just one person living in it." Sandy had also returned to the hall, leaving the bathroom door open.

"I know she used to work out at the motel on the highway, she cleaned the rooms, although you would never know it from downstairs. She hasn't worked since the place burned down. I guess she got a pension or something? I don't really know. As for boarders, that doesn't make any sense. She was so private, eccentric even. I can't believe she would have any one else living here." Ron was sure he was right about this.

"Alright, never mind. Let's just look in the other rooms right now, maybe they'll tell us something more." Sandy moved to the next door and swung it open. Inside was dim, as Ron expected, the familiar heavy drapes blocking out the light. She flipped on the light switch.

The room, painted light blue, the colour of a warm summer sky, held a single bed and a small wooden dresser. The bed was perfectly made, covered with a blue spread, which also matched the heavy drapes covering the window. No other items were visible in the room, no indication of who had occupied the room or when.

Ron was glad to see that there were no mirrors with pictures leaning against them.

Sandy crossed the room to the closet and opened it. The dark empty space held no clues as to the room's occupant either. It was just a dark, empty space. Ron went to the window to open the drapes. He needed the light to enter in order to break the eeriness he felt creeping into him again.

By the time they opened the last door on the second floor, Ron knew what to expect. The only difference between the two smaller bedrooms was the colour of the walls and curtains. This final room had been finished in light pink, everything clean and sterile much like the first one, providing no more clues than the blue bedroom or the bathroom before it had.

Ron left the room as soon as he had seen it, not even bothering to open the curtains. His mind was in over drive. He stumbled to the stairs and made his way to the more familiar, now welcoming, unorganized living room below. At least there he felt both in control and able to think. Sandy followed close behind him in silence, sitting beside Ron on the couch when she arrived in the room.

Ron stood up. "Look Sandy, I need to clear my head. I'm going down to Tim's to grab a bite and a coffee. Do you want to join me?" He really needed to get out of here so he could process everything. At least there had been no more blood, he thought, while he waited for her reply.

"I think I better get back to the station. I'm still on duty. Maybe I could come back later today, after work?" Sandy asked.

She was not really expected back, but she wanted to take things slowly here. She liked Ron and wanted the relationship, if there was to be one, to develop away from the creepiness they had just seen.

Ron shook his head. "I think I'll go back to my own place today. Coming here may not have been such a good idea after all. Even with no heat and water at home, I know what to expect at my own apartment." Ron took a deep breath. He was talking more to himself than to Sandy.

"Do you want to come by there when you're done and maybe we could go out for supper, you know, mull this over?" Ron asked tentatively.

He had turned to face the un-curtained front window. Talking to himself, he shook his head, "Why set up two bedrooms when no one else lived here and as far as I know, no one ever stayed over night? I know I never stayed. In all the years I've been coming here, I've never stayed over night."

"I'll meet you for supper," she agreed. "Maybe your mother could shed some light on this. She must know her own sister better than you. Why don't you talk to her before we have supper? You know, this may not be a police matter, but it certainly is mysterious."

"You're right about that." Ron agreed, turning back to look at Sandy. "Maybe you're also right about my mom, but getting her to discuss anything she doesn't want to could be like pulling teeth. I'll give it a shot this afternoon. Since I don't know where you live, why don't you come by my place around 6? We'll head out somewhere from there." Ron was preoccupied with the mystery of his aunt, but this did not detract from his elation at spending more time with Sandy.

Chapter 6

They left the house together after locking everything up, leaving all the curtains open for the first time in who knew how long. Edith would be mortified, Ron knew, but this was his house now. He would not be entombed.

Ron headed to his mother's house. He was hoping for some answers, but was not really sure he would be successful. Halfway there, while standing on a corner waiting for the light to change, Ron realized he had asked Sandy out on a date and she had accepted. This realization surprised him, how easy it had been and how naturally it had occurred. It made him smile. Maybe something good would happen out of all this chaos after all. He carried on his way with a renewed bounce in his step.

No one was home when he arrived at his mother's. He let himself in with the key he always carried. Half an hour later his mother arrived, surprised to see him there, but clearly pleased as well. While helping her unpack her purchases, placing the milk and eggs in the fridge, Ron jumped right into the questions he had come to ask. Even though he suspected his mother would not likely tell him anything, whether she knew any thing to tell or not, he had to try. 'Nothing ventured, nothing gained', he thought to himself.

Cindy LaChance

"Mom, have you had a chance to think about what we talked about at the hospital?"

"Ron, Edith has always been strange, you know that. How is work going? Have you made plans for your vacation this year?"

It was obvious that she was going to avoid his direct questions, as he had expected. Finally, out of desperation and frustration, he tried another approach. He asked her about Edith as a child, thinking this might be an area she would discuss. He might learn something that would help put some of this puzzle together.

June was clearly not comfortable with this line of questioning either. She had rarely said anything about their childhood together, beyond the fact that she was pretty much raised by Edith. Ron knew that neither of their parents were still alive, but now he needed to know more details; any bit of information that could help.

The story he finally heard surprised Ron, and yet it did not. Mostly he was surprised that his mother told him anything at all. His mother told him that she could barely remember her own mother and believed that she had died when she was very young. Edith, being 10 years older than her, had acted as her mother, cared for her, fed her, played with her and protected her when she needed it. The family, consisting of herself, Edith and their father, had lived in a small two-room cottage on the edge of Lake Erie, somewhere between the areas of Turkey Point and Long Point, she thought. She could not say exactly where the cottage had been located.

The girls, she told him, had shared the one bedroom for sleeping while their father, for the time that he was there, slept on the couch in the kitchen/living area. She could not recall what he did for a living and thought perhaps she had never known.

What she could remember was his anger and his drinking, both a daily occurrence. Even though she had been very young, she said, these two things she never forgot. The girls had not gone to school and had no friends who visited them. Even then, Edith did not talk, which at times would be the source of their father's anger. At other times he would say how perfect a woman Edith would turn out to be, silent and able to cook. He would always laugh maliciously when he said this in some kind of drunken private joke. Even as a child, she knew this comment was intended to hurt Edith.

When June stopped talking about her early life, Ron quietly urged his mother to continue, telling her they only had each other now. He really wanted to know about his family. His mother looked at him with a small smile, reminding him she was his family now. He remained silent.

She reluctantly continued, telling Ron of how the girls would keep them selves occupied while they spent hour after hour alone in the cottage, keeping it clean, cooking, when there was food, playing at the beach and collecting the many shells they found. They had not dared bring them in the house, but rather kept the collection in empty cans in a small shed, which was long deserted, but near their home. They did have one small box of shells they hid in their room. Ron thought of the box of shells and pebbles he had often played with at Edith's.

His mother's face changed suddenly, looking both scared and confused as she mentioned the shed.

She told him that life had changed suddenly for the two young girls, and in her opinion, this had been a good thing. This change occurred one night, she explained, when she had been about five years old. She told Ron about how her father had come home, very late and very drunk as usual. The three ate a late meal because he had remembered to bring home food this time. She said she could recall, to this day, the meal of perch and potatoes, which is why she had never eaten perch again.

What was not usual about this night, she said, was that her father had grabbed June by the arm, pulling her off her feet as he screamed at her in rage. He then hit her in the face and threw her across the floor of the kitchen/living room area. This had occurred after she had accidentally dropped one of the few plates they had in the cabin while she was washing it. As the plate lay in pieces on the floor, he had been awoken from his sleep by the noise. She had never been hit by him before and was petrified as well as physically hurt. She stayed on the floor where she had landed, too scared to move, not knowing what might come next. Experience had told her there was more to come. She had seen it enough with Edith, but all this was new for her.

She knew, even at that young age, that her father had an explosive temper, but usually it was Edith who received treatment of this type. Edith would step in to protect her when her father was angry and drunk by sending June to the bedroom or outside so she was away from his swinging hands and foul mouth.

She could recall many times her sister silently crying in the night after being hit, having bruises and cuts in the morning light, her body heaving as the tears streamed down her face, but still remaining quiet. On those nights, the girls would hold each other.

Ron sat disbelievingly in silence, listening to his mother painfully recalling her childhood to him for the first time. He didn't know what to say, so he sat quiet, processing everything, trying to understand how anyone could treat children in such a way. He just held her hand as she looked away, even as she continued to speak. It was like a damn bursting, everything gushing out through the small hole in the previously impervious wall.

June went on to tell him in detail about the night she was hit, something she said she would never forget for the rest of her life. Edith had run to her, pulled her up from the floor and pushed her toward the bedroom, trying to protect her once again. She had run instinctively, leaving Edith standing behind her, hearing her father yelling, screaming really, at the both of them. From behind the closed bedroom door, she heard more hitting, broken only by the sound of the remainder of the dishes as they smashed against the floor and walls. Her father was screaming about the girls not being good for anything, about them being like wild animals, so, he had stated, they could eat like animals, without plates, off the floor for all he cared.

She had known even then what was happening to Edith on the other side of the door. She did not have to see anything to know. She knew Edith needed someone to help her but June was unable to provide this for her sister. Instead, she remained crouched in the corner of the small room, as far from the door as the small space would permit, her eyes closed as the tears soaked her face, praying only that her father would not open the door.

June stood suddenly and walked to the stove, where she turned on the kettle for tea. Ron had just watched a grown woman reliving the terrors of a small child, every detail evident on her face and in her cracking voice. He had no doubt that everything she said was true.

Turning to Ron, she asked quietly, almost pleading to him. "Are you sure you need to hear things like this, Ron? I've kept this all inside for so long, buried it so I could look to the future, not live in the past." She rung her hands as she spoke.

Ron went to his mother and held her as they stood in the kitchen, waiting for the water to be ready for her tea. With the sharing of her past, both knew that nothing would be the same from this point on. Ron realized he would never again look at his mother and begrudge her when she would not discuss a subject. He could understand now why she had developed this pattern. It explained how this very system of interacting with people, blocking out the negative, had made her into the wonderful person she was.

"Mom, I had no idea. How could any one be so mean to you and Edith, so mean to his two small children? No wonder you never wanted to talk about your childhood. I never meant to upset you, mom. I was just trying to find some answers, answers to explain what was going on with Aunt Edith. I'm so sorry. Are you okay?" The guilt he felt at making her bring back this horrible past, having it infect her kitchen, was enormous.

"Yes, Ron. Actually, as much as it hurts me to bring all these memories back to the surface, in a way it also feels good. What I mean is, I've never really told anyone about my childhood, about that one night in particular." She paused, looking out the window.

"I never even told your father. Obviously Edith never spoke of it, so it lay silently buried between the two of us." She finished the tea preparations and they returned to the kitchen table together, each with their cups held for warmth and support.

"Did your father ever hit you again after that? You said Edith was the one who was usually hit by him." Ron asked gently.

"No, Ron, he never did, and for that I was grateful."

As Ron and his mother sat quietly at the table, letting the tea in front of them cool, the phone rang. His mother reached for it automatically. She spoke briefly, leaving Ron to think on what he had learned.

"Ron, that was Jane, you know, from the bridge club? She's coming to pick me up because we have a couple of errands to run before the game tonight." She patted his hand.

"Regardless of anything, Ron, I want you to always remember how much your father and I both love you. We would never treat you the way my father did. That's why I never really spoke about him before. I think some things are better left alone. Let's drop this for now. I need to get ready to go with Jane. Ron, let's just move on from here, you and I together. Edith is gone, but we still have our lives to live. Let's not do it in the past, okay?" The message was clear. For now, the past was done and he would learn no more tonight.

She stood and kissed him then, leaving him at the table as she went to her room to get changed for her weekly bridge game, as she had done for over ten years.

"But, mom, what happened . . . ?"

"Life went on Ron." She called without turning around. "We'll talk again soon. I know you deserve to have your questions answered, but I can't talk about it any more right now. Some answers I don't even have. I have to get ready now. I'll see you later."

Ron remained seated at the table, thinking about what he had just learned, trying without success to imagine being so small and so scared by the people who are supposed to love you, but he couldn't do it. He had never felt this way himself as a child. He knew it was time to go home. He could hear his mother getting ready to go out. There would be no further conversation today.

Chapter 7

Sandy arrived at his apartment right on time. She had dressed casually in jeans and a light sweater to ward off the chill of the evening. Her eyes sparkled in the light. Tonight her hair was down, hanging in gentle curls to her shoulders.

Ron liked the looked, more so even than when he had first seen her with all that hair pulled back. She had worn flat shoes, he noticed, so he remained a few inches taller than her. Her slim figure looked very nice in the casual outfit. He thought she could dress in a burlap bag and still look great.

"Come on in, I just need to grab my coat." Ron said, when he answered the door. He was glad she had really come by. He had wondered if she would.

"It's a little chilly now, that's why I wore a sweater. I have a coat in the car. Where are you taking me anyway? I hope I'm not under dressed" Sandy smiled at him.

"No, you look great. Your outfit is fine." Ron swallowed hard as he said this, knowing that indeed every eye would be on him tonight with her at his side.

They left quickly, heading to a local Italian restaurant that was both famous for it's pasta as well as the quiet, serene atmosphere. Ron had been many times with friends and knew the owner well. He was pleased to be taking Sandy there tonight.

"Did you get a chance to talk to your mom, Ron?" Sandy asked as they waited at a light.

Ron really wanted to talk about what he had learned from his mom today, but not until they had settled at their table. He knew he was onto a good thing with Sandy and didn't want to scare her away with the weird history he had just learned.

"I've spoken to my mother." was all he said during the drive. He was still trying to process.

The owner, upon arrival greeted them. "Ron, so pleased to see you again. It's been awhile. Follow me to a nice quiet table."

After placing their order, Sandy waited, and then finally asked what his mother had told him that had caused him to be so quiet. Ron told her what he had learned about his mother and aunt, about the grandfather he had, thankfully in his opinion, never known.

Sandy listened patiently, not interrupting. Ron appreciated her for that. He felt even more comfortable with her now. When he had completed the story, he looked into her eyes. She met his gaze.

"What makes people act like that, Sandy? I can't imagine doing something like that to a little child, treating children like that. I don't think I was ever hit a day in my life, at least not that I can remember. All my parents had to do was look at me or lecture me, that's all it took for me to toe the line." Ron shook his head, thinking about what his mother had described.

Sandy sighed, "This is obviously all new to you, Ron. I see this type of thing through my work a lot, people who hurt their kids, just because they can. Sometimes, it seems parents have no idea just how much damage they do." Sandy sipped her wine, reflecting on cases she had dealt with. Ron sat in silence.

"Sometimes, they just get so mad and lash out at who ever is nearby, which is often the kids. The strangest part for me is how those children sometimes feel about their parents any way. Usually they still love them, still want to be with them, probably hoping things will get better, of course, they rarely do." Laughter from another table caught the couple off guard, but the humanity was a pleasant distraction.

"What happened to your grandfather? You said you never met him." Sandy felt for the man across the table. This world he had just learned about was clearly foreign to him. Part of her wished she was still so innocent to the ways of the world, but being a cop prevented that.

"I don't know what happened to him" Ron shook his head. "Mom never got that far in her story. She told me what I've told you and nothing else. I always assumed her father was dead. Since I've never met him, I just always assumed he died before I was born. Mom did say he never hit her again, but not why. At least there is that for her."

Ron smiled at his beautiful date and passed her the bread. Time to move on to more pleasant topics, he thought, before I scare her away for good.

They spent the rest of the evening together talking about their respective jobs, joking, complaining about the politics and rules involved in both, finding out more about each other. It seemed they had more in common than not. They shared a large chocolate desert to finish up the meal, even though Sandy complained that such an extravagance would be hell on her figure. Ron thought no damage had been done.

At the end of the night, they both agreed they had a nice time and would like to do it again. Ron was elated at the prospect, the thought of which over shadowed any concerns he had for his aunt and her strange behaviour. Their easy camaraderie made the night fly by and the prospect of more such nights was enticing.

When she dropped him off, Sandy said she would call him in a couple of days. It was not until later, alone in his now dark apartment, that he realized that she knew both his address and phone number at home but he did not know hers. He of course knew her work number, but that was available to every person in the city by calling the police station.

This was very different for him, this reversal of roles. He realized he kind of liked it this way, leaving the next call up to her. Little did he realize at the time that the next call she made to him was not just about another date.

Chapter 8

Finally, the necessary arrangements completed for Edith, Ron returned to work. He felt he needed to get back into a routine while deciding what to do from here. He was glad to be back in the classroom. The kids could be challenging at times but in a positive way. They kept him on his toes with their daily antics and questions. Although he had never suspected any of the kids he taught were being hurt at home, he kept thinking about his mother and aunt, now looking more carefully at the students he came into daily contact with. Ron was determined to watch his kids carefully for any sign that would suggest one of them might need help. He might even try to incorporate this idea into the classroom; opening up the topic so those who might need help would know they had someone they could turn to.

He had not yet returned again to speak to his mother since she had told him about her early life. He had thought long and hard about what he really needed to know and why he might need the information. Finally he had come to the conclusion that he did not want to make his mother relive any more painful events. He was comfortable with this decision until one day during the afternoon break when he received a call at work from Sandy.

"Ron, are you busy this evening?" She asked. "I've been doing a bit of 'unofficial' checking around and I think we should probably get together to talk. I'm free this evening, how about dinner again?"

"Sure, but what's going on?" Ron was curious. Her tone suggested she had some important information and he assumed it would be about his family.

"I think it would be better if we discuss this in person. Besides, we both have to eat," was all Sandy would say.

Ron agreed to this arrangement, even though he was very curious about what she had found out. He was pleased to be having dinner with her again.

"Why don't you come by my place it's not great but I'll cook for us. That way we can talk in private and not be interrupted. I'm done at four, so let's say around six, will you be off by then?" Ron asked.

They finalized the evenings' plans before hanging up. Ron spent the remainder of the afternoon alternately thinking about what she had to tell him and what he would cook for supper. He finally solved both problems by deciding to be patient about the information and to have a casual dinner of chicken and pasta, which he was sure she would like. At least it was something he knew how to make well. Even with these issues resolved, it was difficult to stay focused for the rest of the school day. He knew today he was probably happier than his young students when the final bell rang.

Silent Secrets

By the time she arrived, the house was filled with the rich aroma of herbed chicken and mushrooms. He had stopped for a bottle of wine on the way home, which he had chilling in a bucket of ice on the table. He offered her a drink as they sat in the living room while supper simmered in the small kitchen. Ron was glad the water and the heat both seemed to be working today. Sometimes life can be good, he thought happily.

"Ron, I can't help being a cop," was Sandy's opening line when they had settled on the couch, drinks in hand. "After what you told me the other night, I was curious. I did some checking through some friends and found out something either your mother may not remember or may not want to share. I thought you would still want to know. I hope I'm right." Sandy took a sip of the white wine in her hand.

"What are you talking about, Sandy? You found out something about me or my mother?" Ron was perplexed, again. He was beginning to feel he would spend the rest of his life in a state of being perplexed.

"Well, actually, it seemed odd to me, what your mother had told you, particularly the part about how she was never again hurt by her father. That's not generally the way things work. At least that's not been my experience. People who abuse their kids believe it's their right. They're not just going to stop for no reason. They usually need to be somehow made to stop. Understand?" She stopped talking and looked at him. Ron just nodded in agreement.

"I began to think about why someone would stop beating on their kids on their own. Maybe it's because I'm a cop, but I could only come up with a couple of reasons. Either your mother and aunt were removed from their father by the authorities, or he died. Do you see where I'm going with this? So I made a friendly call to a friend who in the Lake Erie area, but she could find no information on your family. Then I called the police there. My uncle used to be stationed there for many years. I talked to some of his old friends just to see if anyone could recall a situation involving a couple kids living with their father in a cabin. I figured we were talking early '40's. A couple days later, I got a call back with some information about a man named Jack Jones who had lived there at the time.

"But how did you know his name? I don't even know his name?" Ron asked.

"Well, I didn't know his first name, but on the death certificate, the coroner asked your mother for Edith's maiden name. I used that. It was all I had to go on."

"Oh, yeah, I remember he spoke to mom about that. So what did you find out?" Ron was mesmerized.

"Well, I was sent an old police report, well actually a sheriff then, but a report about a man named Jack Jones. At least that's the name they had on the report based on information given to the sheriff by the locals at the time. Some fisherman had apparently reported a fire in a cabin, near Long Point. The report just said that by the time anyone arrived, the whole cabin was gone. There was no report of anyone being found in the place, but they did find evidence of someone having lived there at some point, likely with kids. They found a few clothing items and stuff like that. No one ever came forward to claim the land after the fire. I think it eventually became part of the bird Sanctuary area that's down there now." Sandy paused, sipping the wine and looking at Ron.

"It only makes sense that this is the right person, the time frame is right, the last name at least is right, the area is right. See what I mean?" Sandy stopped again, looking at Ron.

"So, if that was my grandfather's place, my mother's child hood home, where did everyone go? He and mom and aunt Edith, I mean? Why would the fact that their house burnt have stopped him from hitting his kids? From what mom has already said, this should have just made him angrier." Ron mused.

"Well, maybe before that happened, you know, the place burning down, someone came and took the girls away, someone besides the authorities? That would explain why your mother said she never got hit again. Maybe they had some other family they went to stay with or something like that?" Sandy suggested.

"As far as I know, there are no other family members. But hey, I've been wrong before when it comes to my family. I guess I could ask mom about it, but I don't want to drag up all those old memories for her just to ease my own curiosity." Ron said as he absently stirred dinner.

"Do you know much about Long Point, Ron?" Sandy asked as they sat down to dinner.

"Sure, I guess. I've been there a few times. It's a pretty good beach; there're lots of cottages around for people with boats. I remember there's some kind of bird sanctuary there." Ron replied. "That's about the extent of my knowledge I guess."

"Yeah, okay, all that's true, but there's a lot more to the place than just boats and cottages. The area itself has quite a colourful history." Sandy was clearly in her element with this information. Ron let her talk.

Sandy went on to tell Ron that Long Point was a very busy little area during the Prohibition era. The locals used to sail over to Pennsylvania and back with illegal whiskey in tow. The rules about prohibition didn't match in both countries and with Pennsylvania being so close; there was a lot of money to be made on both sides of the border. The fisherman became very clever at hiding their cargo from the authorities, but of course, accidents happened. Some ships went down in the rough waters, while at other times the crew simply tried to hide the whiskey in the water or along the shore to prevent it being confiscated. For years after Prohibition had ended, people found bottles of illegal whiskey in that area. Some times whole loads buried together. Of course, the bottles weren't always in tact.

"Wow, I didn't know that, but I guess it makes sense, Long Point and Pennsylvania being so close. See, even teachers have things to learn." Ron joked.

"Well," Sandy continued. "I've been thinking about this Jack Jones guy, living down there all alone with his family. I bet he signed himself onto a local fishing boat for employment in the good weather but he probably also spent his free time beach combing for those lost caches of whiskey. That would explain his long absences and his often drunken state when he returned home. Sandy explained excitedly. "Even if he couldn't sell it, free booze is free booze."

Hearing the tale and thinking about a life like that, Ron thought it sounded kind of romantic, like a roving pirate off to find buried treasure long forgotten. Then he remembered about the real life his mother and her sister had lived and realized there was no romance for either of them, just fear, pain and hunger. He did agree though that Sandy's conclusion made sense. It was possible his grandfather either drank his finds or bootlegged the old whiskey for profit in the off seasons of fishing. It was an interesting idea.

Sandy and Ron spent the rest of the evening speculating on what had occurred over 60 years ago, debating all the possibilities they could come up with. They also tried to determine how the long ago events might be related to his aunt and her strange self-abusive behaviour in the privacy of her room.

The wind had shifted outside throughout the evening, bringing a chill to the apartment as the two sat talking the night away. By the end of the evening, in part due to the draft he could feel creeping into his living room, Ron had decided that he would move into his aunts' house. He would clean it up and decide after that if he wanted to stay living there or sell it later. Sandy agreed this was a good idea She thought it was one his aunt would likely have been happy with.

Early the following Saturday Ron was at his aunts', having picked up some boxes to start gathering the clutter before deciding what to keep and what to throw away. His friend had agreed to lend him a truck to haul away what he needed to take to the dump. He was pretty sure there would be plenty enough to fill the pickup and possibly more.

Ron started in the living room, gathering at first all the old newspapers and flyers along with the tattered magazines that were long out of date. He thought briefly about taking the old magazines to the hospital for their waiting room. At least some were newer than the ones he had seen there. Instead, he packed them away to be hauled to the paper-recycling centre. He had initially thought it would be an easy task, but the sorting and packing up took him longer than he had expected.

As he gathered and sorted, he thought about what to do with all the books. Most held no interest for him, being stories of romance and drama. Those could be sent down to the book exchange, some one, he was sure, would enjoy them. As he packed each one, he flipped through it to be sure his aunt had not squirreled anything away between the pages. After all the recent events, he didn't know what to he might find any more. By noon, he had eight boxes packed, most of those contained garbage papers, while the others he sorted separately to be exchanged or donated to the used bookstore.

As he was about to start on the shelf against the window wall in the living room, where the unused radio he had bought sat covered in dust, his mother un-expectantly arrived at the door. Ron was glad she had come by. He had called her several times since he found out about his grandfather's place but she had been unavailable, busy with either her friends or more often, the church. He had asked to her come by the house over the weekend, if she could, to help him with this sorting task, letting her know she could keep anything she thought she might want. Besides the papers, the room contained years of useless knick-knacks that Ron could not imagine keeping. Since she had said she was now feeling better, he thought it would be a good time to tackle the job. Her health was never predictable. Maybe, Ron thought, she would even continue with her story, although Ron was reluctant now to force the issue.

"I'm sure there is nothing here I would want." she stated as she looked at the pile of boxes Ron had already packed. "I'm not the reader your aunt was and those old dust collectors on the shelves were meant for her, not me."

Ron had been thinking over the last couple of days about how and if to approach his mother with the information he had been given from Sandy. He debated with himself while she walked around the living room, trying to decide if it was important enough to talk to her about it or not. Finally, as he watched her moving through the room, absently touching various surfaces, he decided that he did, after all, need to know more, at least a little.

He had also started to think that the photo he had found could be his grandfather, mother and aunt, even though the one child had looked like a boy. Maybe his grandfather had been so mean because he wanted a boy? The ages didn't fit with his mother and aunt, he knew. He wondered briefly if there could have been another sibling of whom he had never heard. His mind whirled in circles but he was no closer to an explanation. Until she had arrived, he had thought he could live without the answers, but now . . .

He was sure his mother could clarify some of this, so he had brought the picture down this morning, leaving it standing alone on the coffee table that was now cleaned of all the other books and papers. His mother obviously saw it as she wandered the room, but neither picked it up nor commented on it. As far as he could tell, she had not reacted to the photograph in any way. Well, it had been worth a shot, Ron thought.

Ron made tea for the both of them. They sat silently at the kitchen table, both quiet for the time being.

Chapter 9

"Mom," Ron finally broke the silence. "I've been thinking about what you told me the other night, about when you were little. You said you were only hit that one time, and that that your father never hit you again after that." Ron paused, hoping his mom would not just stand up and leave the house. She sat silently, staring into the teacup in front of her.

"Do you remember Detective O'Leary from the hospital? She and I have been talking about Aunt Edith and, well, Sandy did some checking. She found out that a man named Jack Jones owned, or at least lived in, a cabin on Lake Erie back around 1942 or so. Is that your father? Did you and Aunt Edith live in that burned out cabin with him?" He also told her about the history lesson of the area Sandy had given him.

Ron could tell by the look on his mother's face that she had anticipated the questions. She knew her son well enough to know that he would never give up until he had all the answers The look also suggested she was surprised by what he had found out so quickly. Maybe she had just hoped he was ready to drop the subject.

"Ron, I'm don't understand why all this is so important to you. It was all such a long time ago and so many things are different now. But if you think you must know, I guess it's time to tell you." She took a sip from her cup before continuing.

"After that night my father hit me, I told you I waited in my room, which I did. I waited a very long time, sitting all alone in the dark. At least it seemed like a long time to me. Eventually, the yelling and smashing stopped and Edith came in to the room. I could see even in the dim light from the window that her face was swollen and bleeding." Ron could see the memory was causing her anguish, her furrowed brows were evident of that. He remained silent, not wanting to interrupt her flow.

"I knew, even being so young, that she was really hurt this time. We lay down on the bed and held each other, as we had so many times before. Shortly, all I could hear was the deep snoring of my father from the other room. He always snored really loud when he was drinking. That I do remember. I had drifted off to sleep to that sound so many times."

"Later, at some point in the night, Edith woke me up. She had a bag in her hand and made me get up, shushing me with her hand. She and I walked down to the shed we always played in, and then Edith motioned for me to wait there." June waved her hands in the air in a sitting motion, mimicking her sister from that long ago night. Ron remained quiet, lost in the story he was hearing.

"She left me there with the bag she had brought. I didn't really understand what she was doing, but I did what she wanted. I sat in the dark and held that bag tight to my chest, afraid to make even the slightest noise. She went away and came back a short time later." June paused again for a sip from her cup. Ron could tell this was very difficult for her.

"Then we started walking in the dark. We walked all night, through the woods and along the shore, until we came to a barn just before the sun came up. I remember that barn like it was yesterday. I was so tired from walking. We slept in that barn for most of the day, hiding up in the hayloft. After all that walking, I fell right to sleep. I think it must have been late spring. I remember the barn was very hot, but we were so tired. We traveled that way for several days, walking at night, away from that cabin. Each morning we'd find somewhere to sleep in the day. Sometimes we found a building, other times we just laid down near the tree line." June paused again, pouring herself more tea from the pot on the table. Ron worried she would stop again, but she did not.

"One day, a man found us sleeping in his barn. He tried to talk to us about what we were doing there, but I was too scared to talk and my sister couldn't, of course. He took us to his house where his wife was. She was very nice to us; she gave us something to eat right away. I guess we must have looked quite a sight by then. When I told her that my sister couldn't talk, she gave her a note pad and a pencil, but Edith couldn't write very well either, so I told them that our parents had died, that we needed some help. I didn't know what else to say. I knew enough to ask if there were any jobs we could do on the farm. The couple agreed that we could stay there and help out with the chores. She let us sleep in the attic and my sister spent the next year cleaning the house and helping out with the other children."

June had a far away look on her face that was both fond and tragic at the same time. Ron reached over to hold her hand.

"That fall I was sent to school, for the very first time, with the other children in the house. Edith didn't go because she couldn't talk. What I remember most about our time there was that no one yelled, no one hit and we ate every day. I once broke a plate. The only thing that happened was it was thrown in the garbage. It might not seem like a lot to you, but to me those things were very important." June stopped talking long enough to take a sip of her tea. Ron sipped his own as well, even though it had long grown cold. Suddenly his mouth was very dry. Ron had never heard his mother talk for so long a time before.

"When I was about eight, I guess, my sister found a real job, a paying job, cleaning the rooms at a hotel. By then she was about 17 years old, I think. Eventually, with the money she had saved, she and I moved to a little apartment close to the hotel."

June smiled now, pleasant memories replacing the terrible things she had already spoken of. "The two of us often went back to visit that family, until the children all grew and we became busy with our own lives. Never once did those people ask for any thing from us in return for everything they had done for us. They saved our lives and expected nothing in return."

"Mom, but what . . ."

"Not now Ron, you promised just to listen. Let me finish while I can." She patted his hand briefly, then folded her hands together in her lap.

"Once we moved, I kept going to school, my sister kept working and we looked after each other. As I learned to read and write, I taught Edith, so she could at least make people understand her. When I met your father, I moved out and the rest, as they say, is history. It was a difficult time, Ron, but Edith made everything work out in the end. I owed her my life, literally, I believe. She was all I had."

His mother looked out into the yard, now in shadows from the late after noon sun. They had been sitting in the kitchen for a long time, Ron realized. When she remained quiet, Ron decided she was finished.

"Didn't anyone come looking for you, like the police or something? Didn't your father try to find you? Didn't anyone wonder who you were?" Ron blurted out his questions quickly.

"I guess I can only say that times were different then, Ron. People looked after each other and made the best of it. Not like today where no one wants to get involved or help out someone else."

"So what about your father? What happened? Why didn't he at least come looking for the two of you?" Ron asked.

"I didn't really know anything until years later. When I was about 18 or so, I started wondering about him, wondering what happened to him and everything, so I asked Edith, but of course she wouldn't tell me anything. I looked in the old newspapers at the library and found a story about the old cabin having burned and no one coming forward about who lived there. I came to believe, based on that newspaper story, that she returned to the cabin while I waited in the shed. Maybe she even set the place on fire. I don't know that for certain, but it's possible."

"Well, I can understand why you would think that. Did Edith ever tell you anything at all?"

"It wasn't until many years later, after you were born, that she finally 'talked' about anything at all. Even then all she would say was that he had killed our mother. She never really explained this to me, but I know that she had never forgiven him for that. She said she wasn't going to let him kill us as well. So I'm pretty sure that she did something, I'm just not sure what. All I know for fact is that I never saw him again." June looked at Ron now. He had more questions but didn't ask them.

"So now you know why he never hit either of us again. I couldn't tell any one. I didn't want to tell any one, about what I thought Edith might have done. She was all I had and he was such a horrible man to us both. I know, if that's what did happen, it was wrong . . ." His mother was looking at him, pleading with him to understand.

Finally Ron had to say something. He had kept quiet as long as he could.

"My god mom, what you two went through. I can't believe this. It's like something out of a movie." He stood and hugged her then, wanting to take away the pain she had kept inside for all these years.

"Do you think it's possible that Aunt Edith was punishing herself because she had done something to your father, even if he was abusive to you? Could that be the explanation for those whippings she endured?" Ron asked quietly as they each sat back in their chairs.

"I've told you so many times, Ron, your aunt was different. She did strange things. Do I think it's possible that she felt guilty about something like that? No, not really, at least I don't think so. Edith put up with a lot of pain from our father before we finally left, but she never really talked about it again."

"What about that picture? Is that your father?"

"No Ron, that's definitely not him. We didn't have enough money for food, so we would never have had a picture taken."

His mother glanced around the room again. "All this is very upsetting for me Ron. I'm not sure how any of this is going to make you feel better. You need to live in the present, not let the past get in the way. That's what Edith and I did and I think you should do the same. If your father were here, he'd tell you the same thing. What's happened is done. We can't change it now. If we live in the present and treat each other well, that's all we need to concern ourselves with." She stood, taking her teacup to the sink.

"I'm going home now, Ron. I'm still not feeling great. These past few weeks have been very hard for me. I'll leave you to finish working here. There's nothing in this house that I want to keep. Just throw everything out. This is your home now, Ron. Make it comfortable and don't live in the past." She dried her hands on the towel by the sink before turning around.

"Mom, look. I didn't mean to upset you. I'm just confused about that picture mostly and Aunt Edith whipping herself." Ron had been about to embrace his mother once again, but instead he let his hands fall to his sides.

"You're right. I need to just get this place cleaned out and start fresh. You go home and rest. I'm sure you'll feel better after a short nap." Right now he was worried about her. This had been a very difficult thing for her to tell.

Ron called a cab for his mother from his newly installed phone and waited with her outside until it arrived. He was about to go inside when Mr. Wells shuffled up the sidewalk. He stopped in front of Ron's house, a bag of groceries held tightly in his arms. It amazed Ron that he could still take care of himself at his age.

"Ron. It's so nice to see you here again. Will you be moving into the old place? It would be a shame to leave it empty; those punk kids would surely break in and trash the place if it were empty. No respect, kids these days."

"Yes, Mr. Wells. I'm moving in. At least for now. It's kind of a big place for just one person, but we'll see." Ron smiled down at the man, knowing the information would please him.

"That's good, Ronnie. You've spent so much time here anyway. Mrs. Wells will be happy. I'll let her know." He started on his way, but Ron stopped him with his next question.

"Mr. Wells. Do you know, has anyone else ever lived here, with my aunt I mean?" Ron asked, thinking it couldn't hurt anything; even though he was sure he knew the answer.

"No son. Not as long as we've lived next door. It's only ever been your aunt. Her husband had run off by that time, so we never knew him. Why do you ask?" Mr. Wells was looking at the young man like he had possibly hit his head or something.

"Oh, nothing. Just curious about why one person would be living in this big place all by herself."

"I'm sure it was the garden that kept her here, son. She always said it was all she had left after her husband was gone. She dearly loved that garden, especially those roses she tended to so carefully. Why, I'd see her out there every day, carefully picking off the dead leaves, tilling up the soil by hand. When the sun shone on those bushes, it was like a sea of red against the back of the house." He waved his free hand as if imitating an imaginary swell of water.

"Mrs. Wells always says how beautiful those roses look. I remember one time your aunt gave her a cutting but it didn't take. I guess there's something in the soil on your side of the fence that brings out the best for those plants. Any way, we do enjoy looking at them over the fence."

Ron agreed the roses were indeed nice to look at in the summer months. He finished his conversation quickly with the old man. With his lack of gardening skills, Ron thought the roses might soon go the way of Mrs. Wells and his aunt.

They said their goodbyes and Ron returned to the task of sorting through the paperwork in the house, all the while thinking about what his mother had said today. He couldn't understand why she had kept this information to herself all these years. More importantly, he was amazed by what he had heard. Two kids, looking after each other and actually surviving. He couldn't imagine kids these days being able to do that, or even him self for that matter, when he had been younger.

By the end of the day, Ron had the living room and dining room somewhat sorted. The books and magazines had been sorted into boxes to go to the recycle centre or to the book exchange. The knick-knacks he had packed separately, he would take these over to his mothers' church for one of their regular yard sales. He wasn't sure yet what to do with his aunt's notebooks, so he just placed them all together on the bookcase below the radio. With the removal of all the other junk, they easily fit.

The two rooms looked better. They were now brighter and less cluttered with this task done, but Ron knew a really good cleaning was necessary. Perhaps even painting the walls to get rid of the dingy feel in these rooms. He wondered when the last time it was that the house had so much light through the windows.

Ron had already decided that he would be using one of the small bedrooms upstairs to sleep in. He didn't think he could use his aunt's room, even though it was bigger and had a double bed. The good news was that those upstairs rooms didn't really need the cleaning that this lower floor did, except of course to clean out his aunts' clothing. He had already decided to pack those up and donate them to Good Will.

Ron spent the following morning loading the packed boxes into his friend's truck so he could take them to where they needed to go. Once the boxes were gone from the room, Ron was pleased with the effect. Again he wondered why she had kept everything, but like his mother had said, she was a little eccentric, so trying to figure out why she did something might be impossible.

Sandy arrived unannounced around noon, bringing with her sandwiches and coffee for the both of them. Ron welcomed her not only because he was pleased to see her but also because he suddenly realized he was very hungry.

The house contained a lot of food, but most of it Ron planned to just throw out. He had no idea how long the items had been in the freezer and since his aunt obviously never threw any thing out, he decided it was safer to start fresh. He already had the fridge unplugged so he could defrost the freezer and get the unidentifiable ice encrusted items out.

"I would have called first, but you haven't told me your new phone number here." Sandy said, as they sat at the now cleared kitchen table. "This place looks so different already. I see all the boxes in the truck outside. Did you find any other surprises?" She asked, tentatively.

"Not yet, and I'm keeping my fingers crossed that I won't."

Ron quickly filled her in on what his mother had told him while they ate. It was easy to talk to her, like they had been friends for years. Ron liked the way it felt.

Sandy was equally amazed by the information about his mother and aunt. "So, your aunt pretty well looked after your mom since they were little. I'm not sure I could do something like that, you know, be that creative and look after a kid as well as myself at that age."

Ron agreed, he thought again about himself as a teenager and knew he had been far to irresponsible then to look after any one, including himself, without the help of his parents.

"Do you think all that has anything to do with what we found upstairs, like maybe she felt she was paying for something, feeling guilty?" Sandy asked.

"I wondered that myself. I still don't know what to think. I can't understand why she would feel guilty about keeping her little sister safe. Their father was clearly a mean, abusive man and Edith made sure they didn't get hurt anymore. I tried to ask more of mom but she shut down. I guess a little at a time is all I'm going to get."

They finished their sandwiches and coffee in silence. A silence, Ron realized, which was not at all uncomfortable.

Sandy helped him pull the frozen items from the freezer. They were so well packed in, it was hard to tell what some of them were, or had been at one time. Ron threw out the loaves of bread and rolls. The other items, some wrapped in paper and some in plastic, he put in the sink to thaw so he could open them later to see what they contained. At this point he wasn't willing to make any bets. With the freezer empty they chipped away at the ice until the space was clear.

Ron glanced over at Sandy as she finished wiping the last of the water from the freezer sides. He liked what he saw and wondered where things might go from here?

"Look, what do you say to getting out of here for awhile and maybe going out for dinner," he asked quickly. He was still playing with the items in the sink, holding his breath, hoping she would say yes. As he waited, he began unwrapping one particularly heavy papered item.

"Sure, that sounds great. I'm off for a couple days now. Why don't I run home and get changed. I'm really not dressed to go out. Shall I meet you back here?"

"Oh my god. Sandy, look at this," Ron gasped as he stumbled back from the sink.

Sandy quickly stepped over to peer into the sink and saw what Ron had found. Sitting on the butchers paper was a small black handgun. Using a potholder from the counter, Sandy carefully picked it up to see if it was loaded. As she opened the cylinder, two shells fell into the sink. Both Sandy and Ron watched as they sank below the shallow water, the sound seeming like an explosion at the unexpected discovery.

"A gun? Why would she keep a gun in the freezer?" was all Ron could manage.

"That I don't know, but I'm pretty sure she didn't plan to ever use it. She'd never be able to get it out with all the ice around it. This thing looks old. I'm not really that familiar with these old guns, but I can probably find out a bit about it." Sandy stated as she retrieved the shells from the water, placing both the gun and the shells on the counter.

Ron said nothing, just continued to stare silently at the unexpected find.

Sandy wrapped everything in a tea towel. "I can try running the serial number, if you want. If it was registered we might be able to find out where it came from, but honestly, someone who keeps a gun in the freezer is unlikely to have registered it. I don't think you'll be wanting to keep this thing around here though, will you?" she asked.

"What would I want with a gun? Can you get rid of it for me?" Ron asked, still stunned at finding a gun in his passive old aunts' freezer, hidden away for who knew how long.

"Sure, I'll take it over to the station for safe keeping, they'll be able to figure out what kind it is. I'm pretty sure it hasn't been used lately, if that's any consolation. If you decide you want it back, we'll get that figured out as well."

Sandy smiled, trying to lighten the now dark mood in the kitchen. "You know Ron, being with you is a new adventure every day." She placed her wrapped package in a bag, planning to transport it to the police station.

"Now, you said something about dinner? Are you still offering or do I make a date with myself?" she asked.

With the gun out of sight, Ron had mostly gotten over his initial shock, a skill he had developed well over the last couple months.

"Yeah, okay. Let's do that. Right now, anywhere but here sounds like a good plan. I know this great little bar and restaurant place, they always have a band, soft rock or blues. We could enjoy the show and get a bite to eat. It's what, about four o'clock now? How about you meet me back here at around seven?" Ron figured that would give him enough time to clean up and get over the shock as well.

"Agreed, my good man. I'll take this package down to the station and be back here all decked out for dinner. See you in a bit."

Chapter 10

Once Sandy had left, Ron spent a bit more time puttering around the kitchen, still thinking about the gun they had found frozen into the recesses of the old freezer.

Unable to come up with any logical explanation, he headed up the stairs to get ready for his date with Sandy. As he climbed the stairs, he thought about all those years he had visited and not ever gone up. If only he had, maybe things would be different, he thought. But then he would not have met Sandy.

How strange, yet wonderful, life turned out sometimes, he mused as he climbed under the hot water of the shower. Just like my parents. If not for her horrible father, my mother never would have met my father and I would not exist.

To philosophical, he decided, letting the cascading water wash away the strains of the day. Tonight he would be spending the evening with Sandy. With any luck, this would be one of many more to come. She really was a great person, they had so much in common and yet were so different, he decided as he dressed for the evening.

The evening turned out to be better then he had expected. The easy listening background of classical jazz and blues passed through the air. The amazing sounds of the saxophone occasionally catching his attention. Although neither of them recognized the name of the singer on stage, they both agreed she had a wonderful voice. Even with the live band, a conversational tone was easy to achieve as they spoke across the table. The relaxing atmosphere and the great food put them both as ease.

They laughed together, talked about their previous relationships, joked about the clutter in Edith's house and contemplated about how and why some people never throw anything out. The only down fall to the whole evening came when they tried to figure out why that gun had been in the freezer.

This latest surprise in the sequence of recent events escaped explanation for both of them. Neither Ron nor Sandy really wanted to speculate right now about how this fit into the already strange life of his aunt.

As the evening wore on, Ron felt better by the minute in the company of Sandy. If he was any judge of character, Sandy was feeling the same way. In fact, he felt better than he had in a long time. Sandy reached across the table at one point and squeezed his hand gently as he mused about Edith and her strange life. A jolt of electricity passed between the two as their eyes met.

Dinner was exquisite, despite the fact that Ron was more focused on his company than the food which lay before him. They shared the chocolate cheesecake for desert over another beer, each trying to make the evening last longer.

By the end of the night, the kiss good night when Sandy dropped him off came easily and felt very natural. Ron had hesitantly leaned toward her before leaving the car and was pleasantly surprised when she reacted in kind.

"Thanks for a wonderful evening, Ron," Sandy said as she returned her hands to the wheel.

It's been a pleasure, Sandy. Have a good day tomorrow at work."

"I'll call you," she said as Ron exited the car.

He hoped it was very soon. Ron slept peacefully that night for the first time in weeks, waking refreshed and ready to tackle the day.

Trying to establish a routine in his new home, Ron spent his days at school and the evenings cleaning the main part of the house, a job that initially seemed monumental. He tried to ensure he did not destroy memories but he needed to get rid of the clutter and garbage his aunt had let accumulate for so many years. He had decided he didn't want to change too much to fast.

Sandy spent more and more time there as well, helping him with both her suggestions and her friendship. Each time they were together, Ron felt happy. Sandy had told him she felt the same way.

Sandy had found out about the gun as well. She said it turned out to be an old 32 caliber, Iver Johnson 5 shot. This meant little to Ron, however Sandy explained that the gun was no longer manufactured and indeed was now prohibited all together because of its caliber, which she couldn't really explain.

"I'm not really much of a gun expert," she explained.

"I hope I never become an expert either," Ron smiled. He had never had an interest in guns and did not want to start now.

Sandy went on to say that her friends at the station had just told her the gun had been very common and very cheap in the 50's and 60's and many of them had been turned in during the Gun Registration Program, since they were of no value beyond possible sentimentality.

Try as they might, neither was able to come up with a reason for anyone to keep a loaded gun frozen in their freezer, but Ron did know that he didn't want it back. Sandy said she'd make arrangements to have it destroyed. Ron decided he would just chalk it up to another bit of strange behaviour for his aunt. At this rate, he thought, strange was definitely in the lead, with normal falling far behind.

After winning the battle with the clutter, Ron had decided to paint the living room a clean white, hoping this would brighten up the room. One evening, he searched the kitchen and shed for paint brushes or rollers but found none. Deciding the items could possibly be stored in the basement, if they were there at all, Ron headed down the stairs, another area, he realized on the way down the dingy stairs, he had not been to before.

He carried a small flashlight, which he used to illuminate the dark musty area. Spiders ran from the light as he slowly moved forward. At the bottom, he found a pull string hanging from the ceiling near the last step. Pulling it, the small bulb swayed from side to side, casting shadows all around. Ron reached to steady the bulb before the motion made him seasick. Even with the dim light, Ron could see this area contained more boxes which he would need to clear out.

Looking around, Ron recognized immediately the contents of the one large shelf to the right as he stood at the bottom; in fact, he nearly knocked the whole flimsy contraption over when he bumped it with his elbow. The shelf contained his aunts canning jars; most of them full from the fruits and vegetables in the yard. This reminded Ron to contact the woman from the Mission who had dropped by just after Edith's death. He would need to tell them this would be the last donation; canning held no interest for Ron, now that his aunt was not here to orchestrate the project.

As he scanned the remaining shelves, Ron could not see any painting supplies. He saw piles of newspapers and magazines here as there had been upstairs, stacked against the walls, leaving little floor space to move around. The area really needed to be cleaned out. If nothing else, the clutter created a fire hazard. Ron thought the area would make a great tool room. Not that he had a lot of tools, but he might some day. He decided to tackle this project the next morning, enlisting the help of Sandy as well as his friend's truck once again. The job didn't look too big and they should be able to load the boxes in short order. It will be one more job done without too much effort, he thought as he gazed around. At least, he grinned, there won't be any frozen guns down here.

Returning to the main floor of the house, he called Sandy. After he explained what he had found in the basement, she agreed to come over the following morning, prepared to work. He was getting very used to her company and was glad that he no longer lived in his small dingy, drafty apartment. Perhaps his mother had been right, living in the present was definitely good for a person.

Sandy arrived in work clothes, old jeans and a sweatshirt. Her dark shoulder length hair was pulled back in a ponytail. Ron couldn't help but think how good she looked, even decked out so casually. He noticed the blue of her shirt brought out the colour of her eyes.

Going through the boxes in the basement was indeed an easy task for the couple. Mostly they were just old papers that had been stored for whatever reason and were shifted quickly by Ron and Sandy to the waiting truck. The two laughed as the truck filled.

At one point, Sandy held up a hand full of old catalogues from one box. "Are you sure you don't want to order something for your winter wardrobe?"

"Yeah, get me one of those plaid jackets, the kids will all stay in class just to laugh at me." The two laughed over the image.

Behind, underneath and beside this collection was another collection of boxes, each one needing to be sorted to determine what they contained. Several just had more of the same old papers and magazines. Several contained old clothing, probably belonging to Edith at some time, which smelled musty and wet. Ron dumped these musty smelling boxes in the truck; none of the items were usable at all, their final resting place destined to be the city dump.

Sandy had declined to opportunity to wear any of the old house dresses they had found, stating they were a little to classy for her usual wardrobe. Ron could not picture her in the frumpy old flowered outfits.

"Hey, look at this." Sandy called out, after opening one of the boxes close to the back wall. "Baby things."

Ron looked over and could see Sandy holding up a small rattle. The box turned out to contain many baby toys, all clearly old but in relatively good shape. Some of the children's books, which had been lying close to the bottom of the box, smelled musty. Ron and Sandy both wrinkled their noses as the small rose in the small area.

"All right, this is getting really weird. Why would my aunt have baby things? She didn't have any kids. Clearly, from what my mom said about her childhood, they didn't belong to either her or Edith . . ." Ron trailed off, looking from the box to Sandy for an explanation. The thought crossed his mind, not for the first time, that he was really glad she was here to help him.

Sandy, still holding the rattle in her delicate hand, looked at Ron. He noticed a dark smudge of dirt on her cheek. A cobweb had caught in her hair. He wished this was all he had to think about. He wanted to reach over and wipe the dirt from her face, but remained frozen in place.

Silent Secrets

While she had no real answers, she threw out a few suggestions. "Maybe she was storing them for a friend? They could have been yours and your mom didn't have room?" She looked from the toys to Ron as she spoke.

"My mom was a great one for donating unused stuff. I can't imagine she would put anything down here and just leave it for years," Ron said as he shook his head.

I don't know, but I think we're back to the questions again. Let's see what else we find and then we'll worry about the answers. Agreed?"

Ron was about to reply when Sandy leaned forward and kissed him lightly on the lips. "Come on, it's just a few toys." Ron squeezed her hand, which still held the rattle.

"You're right. Let's get this done and get out of this stinking basement." The two exchanged a smile and returned to work.

There were more boxes, containing more papers, and more clothing, which they discarded. With two boxes left, they found another cache of toys, which seemed like they might belong to a slightly older child. There were wooden puzzles and building blocks mostly, but also a wooden toy train with cars that came apart. The workmanship suggested it had been hand made.

Neither Ron nor Sandy said a word, simply putting it aside with the first box of toys. The last box contained more clothing, but this clothing had belonged to a little child, likely a girl from the looks of it. Each item had been carefully wrapped in paper and perfectly folded. The items had a slight smell, but clearly an attempt had been made to preserve them in their original condition.

Ron sat on the floor, and looked at the three boxes in front f him. Without a word, Sandy sat down next to him, running her hand gently on his arm. He silently pondered what was in front of him before he spoke. Sandy did not intrude upon his musings. For this he was grateful.

"All right, maybe she had a friend who wanted her to store some things." Ron said when he finally spoke, breaking the silence.

"That's the only explanation. Obviously those clothes weren't mine. They're little girls' things." Ron gently touched the top dress, still covered in the yellowed tissue paper.

"She didn't have her own kids, so that rules out that possibility." Sandy remained quiet, letting him work through his thoughts on his own.

"Do you see any writing on the boxes to say who they belonged to?" Ron asked as he tipped one box to the side.

Sandy turned the box around, looking inside and out for any identifying information. "Nope, nothing here," she said as she set the box back carefully on the ground. They sat in silence, each wondering about the items.

Suddenly Ron stood, "All right," he said, "this is what I'm going to do. I'll take these things upstairs and we'll finish up down here. Then I'll call my mother and have her come over to see this stuff. If she can't explain it or tell me who it belongs to, it'll be junk too." He grabbed the top box, tucking it under his arm.

"This is getting to be way to much." He said in a whisper as he headed up the stairs.

Sandy didn't follow him. Instead she put the last few papers in a bag, giving Ron the space she thought he needed right now.

In the end, they decided to keep only the three boxes of baby items and the jars of canned fruits and vegetables, which had been in the basement. Nothing else was of any value.

"I really expected we'd find some garden tools," Sandy said as they glanced around the cleared area.

"She kept a few items in the shed. I guess she did most of the work by hand. Anyway, there's no paint stuff here, which is what I was looking for in the first place." Ron laughed.

The space was now clear of the fire hazard Ron had been concerned about and ready to be used for something else.

Ron surveyed the area. "Well, at least now I know where the fuse panel is. How did she ever get to the fuse box to change a blown fuse, do you suppose?" They both laughed at this, breaking the tension that had settled in the air between them.

Ron and Sandy stood in the kitchen after taking the last bag of papers to the truck by the curb. Both were glad the job was done.

"I think that's enough dungeon work for one day. I'll get a shop vac to clean up all the cobwebs, unless you want to collect more with your hair?" Ron joked as he pulled the web from her head.

"Oh, now you think I'm your char woman, do you?" Sandy laughed as she brushed her head for any other webs, which may have been caught there. Ron assured her he had no plan to hide her away in the basement.

"At least now, after all the jars are gone, I'll be able to put my left over paint down here without worrying about the whole place going up in smoke from all the papers. Let's grab a coffee and sit out on the back porch for some fresh air and sunshine. I think we need it after that dark, dirty job." Ron suggested with a smirk on his face.

The air was cold but the sun made the porch a great place to be. The leaves had all fallen now from the large pear trees and other smaller trees leaving the branches bare. The garden, with the exception of the few resilient weeds, which refused to die off from the frosty night air, lay empty. Soon the snow would cover even the hardiest of the weeds for several months.

As they sat, Ron said, "Maybe I'm reading to much into those boxes. She was probably just storing them for someone, like you said, and they just forgot about them. Who knows?" It seemed possible but Ron didn't believe it. "Let's talk about something I can figure out." Ron suggested. Birds, the few that remained, sang in the bare branches of the garden.

"I'm not sure what I'll do with the garden and all the pears next year. I certainly don't want to can them and give them to charity like Aunt Edith obviously did." Ron mused looking out over the back yard.

"Maybe I'll just flatten that garden area down and grow grass over there. What do you think, Sandy?" Her opinion was important to him, regardless of the subject. He hoped she was still around to help with that task next summer.

"Well, maybe you could plant just a few things. Gardening is good for the soul, they say." She reached over and patted his chest.

"As for the pears, you either eat them or rake them up along with all the wasps, so what ever you think on that one. I don't really like pears and I really don't like being stung." Ron grabbed her hand and held it in his own as she gazed at the pear tree.

"I remember one time when I was small. I was picking up fallen apples with my brother. I got stung ten times at least, so don't ask me for any help with that job when the time comes." Sandy laughed, squeezing Ron's hand. She noticed the sun made his blond hair shine.

"The roses are really nice though. Do you know what kind they are?" Sandy asked, pointing to the now bare bushes beside the porch.

Ron turned to look at the bushes, which grew so close to the house. "No, not really, except that they're all red. They do flower really well, though. Aunt Edith spent a lot of time tending those, making sure there were no bugs, covering them with burlap in the fall. I guess I better do that too so they don't get damaged when the snow falls. I think I saw some burlap in the shed."

"Like my father always says, when you own a home, the work never ends. Poor baby," Sandy joked.

Ron had not commented on it, but he had certainly noticed how Sandy had talked about the pears for next year as if she would still be around then. If that were the case, he wouldn't mind picking them all up himself while she sat on the porch.

Ron leaned toward her, intending to kiss her, as the sound of his mother's voice came from inside the house. He smiled at Sandy and squeezed her hand as they both stood to greet his mother.

Regardless of what he had thought in the past about not needing to know more about his aunt, the discovery of the boxes had changed all that.

Ron introduced his mother and Sandy again. They all moved to the living room, which seemed very large and clean now. He wanted to show June the items they had found in the basement. The photograph from Edith's room, the beginning of all the mystery, remained on the coffee table.

"Ron, I hope you didn't ask me to come all the way here just to look at some old garbage you found." June said as she took off her coat. "I already told you I don't want anything that might be here." She sat on the only chair in the room, as she glanced.

"I do like the way you've cleaned up though. It looks so much better, more like when we first moved here, without all that garbage lying around."

"Sandy and I have been working really hard to clean everything" Ron said as he and Sandy sat on the couch, the boxes from the basement at their feet.

"I don't know what ever got into Edith to keep so much stuff." June stated absently as she smiled at her son and his girl. The two look good together, she thought.

Ron watched his mother carefully. He saw her sitting on the edge of her chair, her hands clasped tightly together. It seemed that his mother appeared nervous, but he couldn't figure out why that should be.

"Mom, Sandy and I found these boxes in the basement." He said as he pointed to the three boxes on the floor. His mother followed his gaze but remained quiet.

Ron opened the one nearest him. "Look, baby clothes and toys. Do you know who they might have belonged to? Was Aunt Edith maybe storing them for some one?" Ron watched his mother carefully as he asked the question.

I don't have the slightest idea what your aunt kept or why." The answer was curt. June picked at a thread on the chair arm.

Ron looked at Sandy, but she remained quiet. This was not the time for her to intervene, she had decided. Ron tried again.

"It just seems really strange and I was hoping you would be able to help me out with this. If we know who they belong to, we could return them." Ron watched his mother for a moment. She maintained his gaze but remained silent.

"Can I get you a coffee or something, mom, you look like you're shivering?"

"A cup of coffee would be good, Ron, let me help you with that. I do have a chill, it's rather cold outside today with that north wind. I'm sure we'll see snow before month's end." The discussion of the boxes had been dismissed.

His mother made her way to the kitchen where the coffee pot still held plenty of hot coffee. She kept herself busy for a few minutes, making her own coffee and offering to make coffee for the others Neither Ron nor Sandy wanted coffee. June sat at the kitchen table, her hands wrapped around the steaming cup in front of her. Ron and Sandy remained standing at the counter.

"Why don't you just throw that stuff out, Ron? If it were so important to Edith, she wouldn't have had it in the basement."

"I know, mom, I just thought it might belong to some one who would want it back"

"It's no use to you, donate the toys to someone. Kids always like toys, no matter how old they are. The rest should just be put out with the trash, like most of the stuff in this old place. Why don't you just call that place that took all your old furniture from the apartment and have it done with?" His mother, ever practical, had ignored the plea to find the owners of the boxed items. Sandy nudged him toward the table.

Ron now sat opposite his mother, leaving Sandy standing alone by the sink. "You know mom, we've been through a lot together, you and I. Now there is only the two of us. I don't want to cause any grief for any one, most of all you, but don't you think it strange that Aunt Edith would have baby items in the basement, toothbrushes upstairs, and two rooms perfectly kept that no one ever used. I understand she was a pack rat and that explains the down stairs, but it doesn't explain the upstairs and definitely doesn't explain the picture and her using that whip we found. I just want to have some of this make sense. Can you understand that?" Ron reached over and held his mother's hand across the expanse of the table.

"Ron, I think we've both come to realize that there is a lot about Edith that neither of us knew. What we do know is that she loved us dearly and would do anything for us. She cared for you the same way she cared for me as a child. What's important is that we remember that, remember how much she meant to us and forgive her for her strange behaviours that might not seem to make sense to us now. She had a hard life . . ." His mother trailed off, not finishing her thought, absently picking at the crumbs on the table.

Ron glanced over helplessly at Sandy, who just shrugged her shoulders and remained silent. This was not her place and not her mother, she could think of no way to help Ron, as much as she might want to. Ron continued to hold his mother's free hand until she pulled it away to drink from her cup.

"Okay mom, you obviously don't want to talk about this. I'm just going to put those things in one of the closets upstairs. Maybe someday I'll figure out an answer." Ron stood now; a little miffed his mother was being so evasive once again.

"Do what ever you like with it Ron. I really have to run now. I'm having the girls over for bridge tonight and need to get the place ready. Call me a cab, will you dear, please?" June stood, waiting for her request to be followed.

Ron left to make the call from the phone in the living room. Sandy stepped toward June and held out her hand. "I'm so glad to meet you again, Mrs. Walker. I'm sure Ron is just trying to make sense of everything, not trying to cause any trouble for anyone." It was the best she could do with the awkward moment.

"No dear, Ron would not want to cause trouble for anyone. I'm glad you two have become friends. He's a nice boy. Sometimes it's just hard for him to know when to let things be. I had to learn that a long time ago and I've never regretted my decision for a moment. Maybe you can help Ron with that." The two women smiled at each other as they waited for Ron.

Ron returned and the three went to the front hall to wait for the cab, which arrived in only a few minutes. As the cab pulled away, Ron and Sandy returned to the living room in silence.

Finally Sandy said, "Look Ron, how about I go get a few groceries and I'll make you a special dinner to celebrate the 'cleaning of the dungeon'?"

Ron agreed to the plan. While she was gone, he carried the three boxes upstairs. In the small pink bedroom, he carefully placed the boxes on the shelf in the closet and closed the door. Another mystery tucked away, just like the mirror, which had now been cleaned and stored in the hall way closet. While he waited for Sandy to return, he also placed a call to the Mission to ask if someone could come by the following day if possible to get all the jarred food. He explained this would be the last donation and this year he did not want the jars back. He planned to use that space to store some tools and other household items and certainly didn't want the empty jars taking up the space.

By the time Sandy returned, he had set the dining room table and placed a candle in the centre. Special meals had always been held in the dining room at this mothers' home, and Ron had decided this was to be a special meal. A nice quiet candle lit dinner was in order. He wanted everything to be perfect. At least what he had control over.

Chapter 11

Sandy turned out to be an exceptional cook. She presented Ron with glazed pork chops sitting on a bed of wild rice, baby carrots, diced mushrooms and onions. They started with a Greek salad, something Ron had not had before. The aroma filled the house.

"Wow, this is fantastic, Sandy. Not only are you beautiful, you can cook too." Ron leaned forward and kissed her across the table.

Sandy laughed, returning his kiss. "I have to agree with you, I've outdone my self with this creation." Playfully she touched his nose with her finger.

Over dinner, she explained that she had never really done much cooking growing up. Her mother had prepared all the meals for the family and learning the skill had not interested her. Even after she had moved out on her own, her hectic schedule, combined with her lack of skill in the kitchen, didn't allow much time or desire for home cooking.

"You probably did the same thing I did." Ron smiled.

"When I was hungry enough, I went home." The two laughed at this.

Sandy said that about two years ago, she had decided to enroll in a cooking class on a whim. She needed a distraction from work. She had realized quickly then that she had a knack for creating some pretty good meals.

"I ate great as a kid but now I realize meals had been basic meat and potatoes. Now I really enjoy trying new things. I hope you really do like it." Sandy smiled, casting her eyes to her plate.

Ron was glad he had made one of the few meals he was good at when he had cooked for her. "If this is any indication of what you can do, you're welcome to dinner every night." Ron took the last scrap from his plate, rubbing his stomach as he savored the morsel. Sandy swatted his hand and laughed at him. Ron hoped he really could leave most of the cooking to her.

The next day, Ron and Sandy hauled every one of the jars, about two hundred in total, up to the front hall, neatly stacked in boxes to make them easier to carry. Taking the last few jars from the bottom shelf, Ron accidentally bumped the back panel. The entire rickety shelf looked like it would fall over, much like when he had bumped it during his first venture to the basement. Both Sandy and Ron reached to steady the shelf at the same time, preventing the six-foot unit from falling on their heads.

"Looks like I better fasten that to the wall a little more securely before I put anything else on there." Ron said.

"Well, I'm not standing here forever holding it up," Sandy laughed.

"Maybe I'll move it over to the other side, more out of the way of the stairs. I've already bumped into it one to many times. Well, that's the last of them." Ron stood back with two jars in his hands. He surveyed the area, proud of the work that the two of them had completed.

"I'll wait upstairs for the Mission driver to arrive, if you want, while you get that shelf stable. We don't want it falling over, making bumps in the middle of the night." Sandy smiled at Ron as she headed up the stairs with the last box tucked under her arm.

Ron watched her going. It felt like they had been together a long time. He wanted to ask her to stay over. Maybe she had been thinking the same thing with her comment about the bumps in the night.

As he grabbed the sides of the shelf, it pulled easily away from the wall. Ron slid it sideways, turning at the same time so he could maneuver it into place on the larger opposite wall. Once there, he tied it to another beam, holding it temporarily until he could get back with some screws and brackets that would fix it securely. At least now, it wouldn't fall over in the middle of the night.

As he passed the spot where the shelf had been, he could see the beams of the wall had large boards covering one area. He wondered why this had been done. As Sandy was coming back down the stairs, he called out to her to bring the hammer from the kitchen. Mysteries were no longer a big thing to him and he decided to see if this was going to be another one. Sandy returned quickly with the hammer, expecting he needed it to either move the shelf or keep it in place.

"Ron, what's that?" She asked as she passed the hammer to him. "It doesn't look like it belongs there. Maybe there's an old window behind there." She suggested.

Ron started to remove the rusty nails from the upper boards just as the phone rang. Sandy ran to answer it.

"That was your mom, Ron. She wants to know if we could go over for supper this evening." Sandy came down another step. "June said she had cancelled her bridge game and would like us to come over together."

Ron stopped what he had been doing. "She cancelled her bridge game? Something must be up. I don't remember her ever doing that before. She wants both of us to come?" Ron could not believe what he had heard.

"That's what she said" Sandy said, remaining on the step, waiting for his answer.

"That doesn't sound like mom."

"I don't have to go if you don't want me to." Sandy said. "But she seemed insistent. I said you'd call her right back." Sandy started back up the stairs.

"No, I do want you to go, it's just a little unusual for my mom to cancel her card game. She hasn't done that in all the years I've known her, except once when my father died. I'll call her right back and tell her we'll both be there, okay? This board can wait for another time. Right now I'm more curious about why mom would cancel her beloved card game." Ron placed the hammer on the shelf and left the basement.

"Mom." Ron said when his mother answered the phone, "Is everything all right?"

"Yes Ron, everything is fine. You and Sandy come over around 6 for supper. See you then." Before Ron could say anything, she hung up, preventing Ron from making any further inquiries.

Sandy went home to change while Ron showered. He thought again how nice it would be if she could just change here. By the time she returned, his curiosity had increased. He was feeling very anxious about dinner tonight and almost wished he had not agreed, even though he could not explain why. This seemed to be happening more than Ron wanted. At least, he thought, I'll have Sandy with me.

"Don't worry about it Ron. What ever is going on, you'll know soon enough. Let's walk over to your mom's place, it'll help clear your head." Sandy suggested.

They headed out, hand in hand with no conversation between them. Sandy didn't know Ron's mom well enough to understand why the invitation seemed so odd to him. Her own mother often called to invite her to dinner, usually just leaving a message on her answering machine telling her to come over.

Ron knew his mom well enough to know it was very strange indeed. Supper company on a bridge night? Never. He was lost in thought about what else might happen to throw his world upside down while trying to mentally prepare himself at the same time. The warmth of Sandy's hand in his invaded his thoughts, sweeping him with a calm for the night ahead. Ron knew he could deal with anything if Sandy would just hold his hand and help him through.

When they arrived, his mother had the dining room table set with three places. The smell of roast beef and onions filled the air. This was one of his favourite meals, usually served on Sundays when he had been a kid. Something was definitely going on for her to make this meal on a weeknight.

"We're eating in the dining room, mom?" Ron asked incredulously.

"Yes dear. I use it so infrequently these days; I thought it would be a nice change. Why don't you cut the roast while Sandy and I put the rest of the food in these bowls." She moved the dishes to the table, Sandy joining her without comment, just a shrug to Ron.

She looks okay, Ron thought to himself, but he knew something was wrong, he just couldn't put his finger on it. He focused his attention on the meat, making thin even cuts, the way his father had taught him. The women had the rest of the meal laid out by the time he brought the platter to the table, placing it at the end within easy reach of every one.

"Well, Sandy, I'm so glad you've joined us. Ron seems to have made a very good friend in you." June stated when they had all been seated.

The remainder of the meal was consumed with small talk about Sandy and her job, Ron and his students and the ever-impending coming of winter. The conversation appeared vaguely directed on purpose.

Ron struggled to eat the meal. Even though it tasted delicious, each bite kept sticking in his throat as he waited for the other shoe to drop. 'Just relax,' he told himself, maybe she just wants to get to know Sandy. Maybe she was feeling lonely. None of these ideas really struck Ron as true, but they at least let him finish his meal. When the table had been cleared, they moved to the less formal kitchen table to have coffee. When this had been poured and they were all seated, his mother looked at both Sandy and Ron.

'Here it comes', was all Ron could think.

"Ron, I've been doing a lot of thinking since Edith died. I know a lot has been happening for you as well. You and I have said several times that we only have each other left, and so we do, but you have Sandy now and I asked her to join us tonight because I'm hoping that she will be the good friend to you I believe she is. I want to tell you something, but I need you just to listen. Don't interrupt me and don't ask questions until I'm done. This decision to talk has been very hard for me. Can you promise me that?" His mother was looking at Ron, occasionally glancing over at Sandy.

"Mom, are you sick, is that what's going on?" The thought scared him and yet explained so much. Ron reached for her hand across the table, but she pulled it away.

"Ron, I'm not sick, nothing's wrong with me, at least nothing new. Can you just listen quietly and let me talk? I've made up my mind but I can only do this once." She waited for his reply.

"Of course, mom. Please tell me what's going on." Ron pleaded, also looking at Sandy for guidance. She reached out for his hand.

His mother sat back in her chair, folding her hands on the table in front of her. She looked to the ceiling, then back at Ron. Sandy continued to sit quietly beside Ron, holding her coffee cup, but not drinking the still hot liquid. Even she knew something important was about to happen.

"Ron, a long time ago, Edith met a wonderful man who thought the world of her. They met when he stayed once at the motel she worked for. He kept coming back to the coffee shop to try to talk to her. He was immediately taken with her, but she was very shy around him, around anyone actually." Ron sat silently and listened to the long ago tale.

"One day," June continued, "when I was at the coffee shop there having lunch with her, he introduced himself to me and asked nervously if he could talk to me. He said he had seen me sitting with Edith on several occasions and wanted me to convince her to go out with him. He told me he wanted to get to know Edith more, but she kept ignoring him. She wouldn't talk to him or even give him the time of day, as he put it. He complained that whenever he talked to her, she just smiled and walked away. June smiled at this as she took a sip from her cup.

"I realized then he didn't know she was mute. I explained this to him and he never batted an eyelash. When he and I finished talking, he left the coffee bar and walked immediately across the street to the variety store. I thought he had probably changed his mind about trying to get a date with someone who couldn't talk." June looked at Sandy for a second before continuing.

"I couldn't have been more wrong. Instead of running for the hills, as we used to say, he came back and handed a little black notebook to my sister, who by that time had come to sit with me during her break. He asked her if she would have dinner with him that evening after work, telling her to write her answer in the book while he went to the counter to get a fresh coffee. When she opened the book, we both saw he had written his name on the first page, along with the word Dinner, followed by a question mark. I remember thinking that was so romantic." June smiled at the memory. Ron remained quiet, as he had promised.

"Life was never the same for Edith or me after that. Edith and Joseph, that was his name, seemed to be a match made in heaven. Edith and I had been living in a boarding house, but 6 months after that first date and that first notebook, Edith and Joseph were married. All three of us moved into the home you are in now. Joseph never objected when Edith said I would be moving in as well."

"Mom,?" Ron started but did not get to finish.

"Hush, Ron. Let me finish. The little pink room at the front of the house was mine; at least it was pink then. I remember how excited I was to have my own place, somewhere I could stay and not worry about who was moving in beside us or whether we could pay for the room at the end of each week. I felt safe in that little room, like I had never felt safe before. Of course it didn't last long, the security of that little room. But while it did, I'll never forget it. I was married myself just over a year later and moved out to live with Austin in our first home."

June paused again to take a sip of the coffee before her. Sandy glanced from Ron to June, but remained as quiet as Ron.

"While I was with Edith and Joseph, life was wonderful. Joseph made Edith smile every day, which was wonderful to see. She had spent so many years not smiling at all. He was always bringing small gifts home to her, flowers or candy, stuff like that. Even better, he always made sure she had a little note book to write in." His mother stopped talking and glanced again at both Sandy and Ron, the memories of those long ago days evident in her eyes.

"About six months after they were married, while I was still living there, Joseph brought a lawyer to the house one evening. That lawyer sat with Edith and Joseph in the kitchen, but I could hear what was being said. They were making out an agreement about the house. His own parents, upon their deaths, had given Joseph the house, and he told her he would be putting it in Edith's name now. He kept telling her that it was important to him that she feel this was her home forever and he never wanted her to feel like she would have to leave for any reason. He was so silly in love with her. I think he was afraid that she might, for some reason, decide he wasn't good enough for her or something like that. Of course, I didn't hear Edith say anything during this meeting but that lawyer left shortly after and a stack of papers remained behind on the table." June gestured with her hands as if the papers sat before her now.

"After that I moved out myself, a newly married woman ready to take on the world, or at least I thought that at the time. Before I left though, Edith came to my room one evening and told me she was pregnant. She hadn't told Joseph yet and wondered what I thought he would feel about having a baby. She was so excited and nervous at the same time. I told her I thought he would be very happy." June smiled at sandy again, as if sharing a secret with her alone.

"Later, from the kitchen, for the first time since I had known Joseph, I heard him yelling. The yelling I heard was Joseph, so excited at the idea of a baby, he could hardly contain himself. Sitting in my room upstairs, I could imagine he had picked Edith up and swung her around. That would be something he would do." June smiled at the memory.

Even though Ron had promised to be quiet, he couldn't contain himself any longer.

"Mom, I don't understand. You said before that Aunt Edith didn't have any children, did something happen to that baby, did she lose it?" He was enthralled with the story she was telling, thrilled to finally be learning so much about his aunt. Looking over at Sandy, he knew she felt the same way.

"Ron, let me tell things in my own way. I'm hoping you will understand everything when I'm done. Yes, I did say Edith didn't have children and you'll hopefully understand all that as well if you'll just give me time." June patted his hand.

"Where was I? Oh, yes, when the time came for the baby to be born, Edith would not go to the hospital. She said she was having her baby at home. We called in a nurse and I lived only a couple blocks from her at the time with Austin. Joseph came to get me when her time was near. She had a beautiful baby boy. The most beautiful baby I had ever seen." June gazed at Ron, then Sandy. Both could see the faraway look in her eyes, as if she was back in that house with the baby just arrived.

"Edith and Joseph were so ecstatic. They had fixed up the other bedroom upstairs as a nursery and soon that little boy took over the whole house, as only a baby could. Joseph continued to shower Edith with his little gifts, only now he included his son in his unexpected surprises. I think he was the best husband and father Edith, or anyone for that matter, could have ever wanted. Joseph cared only for his little family. That wonderful little boy was joined two years later with a little sister, again born at home and in perfect condition. Edith, in her strange ways, refused to go to the hospital once again. Joseph and Edith doted on those children but were very good about sharing them as well. Your father and I would often take one or the other for a day or two, to give Edith a break. Since I had no children of my own, I got the chance to enjoy their youthful antics."

His mother stopped again, picking up her coffee cup for a drink, then realized it was empty. She was smiling at the long ago memories. Sandy jumped up quickly to refill all three cups, while Ron looked at his mom in silence, not wanting to interrupt this unprecedented dialogue. It took all his will power to remain silent. June remained quiet herself as the cups were filled.

Finally, Ron couldn't help himself, once again breaking his promise of silence. "Mom, you sound like you're describing the perfect family, and yet Joseph left Edith high and dry. Did he take the children when he left as well, is that what you're saying?"

Ron had known his whole life that Edith had once been married and her husband had left. The children were new information. They had to have left with their father. There was no other explanation.

His mother did not respond; she just smiled and reached for his hand. When Sandy had returned to her place at the table, his mother let go of his hand and took a small sip of the freshly poured coffee.

"Edith and Joseph made a very good family for those children. One day I came over to pick up her son, planning for him to spend the weekend with Austin and I. We wanted to take him on a picnic, the wonderful summer weather made it a perfect time to go down to the beach and enjoy the day. His sister was still too small for such an activity, but I just knew a little boy would love to play in the sand, building castles and finding shells." June became quiet. It took all Ron's willpower not to interrupt.

Finally she continued. "We had our day at the beach and had just returned home, with a very sleepy boy, when Edith showed up at our door. She was very upset, but all she would write was that something terrible had happened. She wrote that Joseph and Emily, that was her daughters' name, were both gone. I had no idea what she was talking about, but she kept pointing to the paper where she had written that I had to keep her son; that she didn't want anything to happen to him. Austin and I tried to calm her down, tried to get her to explain more, but all she would tell us was that she needed to make sure nothing happened to her son as well. As strange as she might have been before that day, she was beyond consoling. The look in her eyes was wild. She left and told us to keep her son safe." June placed her hand on her chest, as if making a promise.

"I went to see her the next day and the day after that, but she never answered the door. I don't know if she was home or not at the time. Finally, a week later, I caught her at home, in the garden. She would only indicate that Joseph and Emily were gone and that from now on her son needed to stay with me." Now she became silent and reached for Ron's hand. She gazed at him, her eyes pleading for him to understand.

"She made me promise to love him always and to bring him to see her as often as I could. Ron, do you understand what I am telling you?" She looked at Ron, then at Sandy.

Ron sat quietly, unable to voice what he thought he had just learned. He looked between his mother and Sandy and back again.

"Am I that boy?" was all he could manage to whisper.

"Yes, Ron. Edith made me promise to love you, but I would have done that anyway. I never really wanted to tell you all this, but since Edith died, you've been asking so many questions and I don't want to lie to you. We only have each other. Maybe now, some things will make sense to you. Like why Edith left you the house, a gift from Joseph to her and now to you. The baby things you found belonged to you and your sister. That picture you found upstairs is you, Emily and Joseph. It was taken just before that day on the beach. I remember Joseph had it taken one day and gave it to Edith as a gift. He was so pleased with it." June wrung her hands, looking from Ron to Sandy as they both sat in silence.

"I'm sorry I didn't tell you all this before Ron, but I didn't know how or when." His mother sat back again, folding and unfolding her hands nervously on the tabletop.

Ron had no idea what to say. Thoughts stampeded through his brain faster than he could process them. He had a sister; his mother was his aunt and his aunt was his mother; his beloved father was his uncle. His father was a man he did not know. He stood and walked to the sink, holding the counter for support, staring into the empty space, trying to think straight.

"Mrs. Walker . . ." Sandy started.

"Please dear, after making you hear about our family secrets, I think you should call me June." She smiled at Sandy then, clearly nervous.

"Okay, June. What happened to Joseph and Emily?" Sandy asked.

"That, my dear, I can't answer for sure. After Ron came to live here, Edith would never again talk about either of them. She just wanted to see Ron to make sure he was being taken care of. She became quite a different person after that, very reclusive. Only wanting to work in her garden and be by her self in that house. She did go back to work at the motel, but she was never the same." June Walker looked over at the man she had raised and who now stood hopelessly puzzled in the very kitchen he had grown up in.

Silence enveloped the room like a blanket. No one moved. Finally Ron returned to the table, sitting down heavily.

"I have some questions, mom. I really need you to answer them for me as honestly as you can. Do you know where Joseph and Emily went or where they are now?" He was not yet able to think of this man Joseph as his father.

"No, Ron. We never heard from them again. I always wondered what could have happened. Everyone assumed that he had run off, because that's what Edith said, but I never believed that my self. I saw him with you and Emily. I saw him with Edith. He was a very happy family man. Not once did he give any indication that he would just leave everything that seemed so important to him." June sounded adamant about this.

"How could two people just disappear? Didn't anyone report them missing, didn't anyone report that Emily might have been kidnapped?" Ron was getting more confused.

"Ron, I'm sure I can never get you to understand. Edith was so insistent that we take you and raise you. She insisted that we leave everything else alone. I didn't know what else to do. All I could think of was that something had happened to Emily, but I didn't know what. I wanted to make sure that you were all right. I know that doesn't make any sense to you." His mother struggled with every answer.

"June, how is it that Ron has your last name and not Edith and Joseph's? Did you adopt him from Edith?" Sandy's police skills kicked in. There were a lot of missing pieces that she thought June probably did have the answers to, even if she didn't realize it.

"No, he's not actually adopted, Sandy." June looked at Ron. "Edith had never legally registered either of the children after they were born, who knows why. Another example of her strange thinking, even then, I guess. When you came to live with us, Ron, we just sent away for the paper work. I put Austin and me on the forms that said we were your parents." She smiled at him now.

"Remember you had been born at home, without the assistance of anyone except Joseph and me. Edith absolutely refused to go to the hospital or even a doctor. You know, she was just as afraid of hospitals then as she was in her later years. There were no hospital or doctor records to dispute who your parents were." June fell silent for several minutes.

"Ron, your father and I just wanted what we thought was best for you. We knew Edith was not right in the head when she came that day. Even though we didn't know what had happened to Emily and Joseph, we did know one thing. We didn't want anything to happen to you." June tried another sip of her coffee, but returned it to the table without actually having a drink.

"Are you saying that she did something to cause Joseph and Emily to leave? Do you think she caused some harm to them?" Ron asked quietly, his mind spinning with a million questions all at once, a million possibilities of what had occurred all those years ago.

"I don't know what to think, Ron, and I never really did. Part of me never wanted to find out for sure. Your father and I talked about that many times over the years. We wondered, if she had done something to them, you know? I think it's possible, and yet, she and Joseph were so much in love. It didn't make any sense to me then and still doesn't now."

June gazed at Ron, then out the window into the dark back yard. The quiet over took the room with only the humming of the kitchen clock intruding on the silent trio. Finally June reached out for his hands again. He crossed the room to her. He returned to his seat, his mind reeling.

"Ron, I know this is all very confusing to you. I know we might have been wrong for what we did, your father and I, but we wanted to care for you, to make sure you were safe. We tried to be good parents to you. Your dad and I have always been very proud of you and I hope what I've told you tonight won't change how you feel about us. There have been so many times over the years we talked about telling you this, but we were scared. We didn't want to lose you after all these years." June stated, tears brimming her eyes.

Ron could see the tears in his mother's eyes and reached for her across the table. As they embraced, he was filled with wonderful memories of his life with this woman and her husband. He knew absolutely that nothing would ever change how he felt, the love and respect he had always had for this surprisingly strong woman. Nor would anything change how he felt about the man he knew as his father.

What he was thinking about now was Joseph and Emily. He couldn't yet think of these people as family, they were just names and faces from an old photo. He was very curious about what had happened so long ago, changing not only his life, but also all the relatives he had as well.

Sandy stood, "Ron, June, maybe I should go. You two probably have a lot to talk about."

June shook her head. "No Sandy, I'm not sure I have anything else to say for tonight. This evening has been very difficult for me and now I think I need some sleep. Why don't you two go out? I'm sure Ron needs someone to talk this over with and I think you're just the right person to help him through this." She smiled at Sandy, then at Ron. The tears remained standing in her eyes, the light reflecting on the unfallen droplets.

June sat back in her chair, releasing Ron from their embrace. She folded her hands in front of her on the table. Looking at her, Ron recognized this look; he knew the conversation was over for tonight.

Although he still wanted to know so much, he did agree that he needed to process the information he had so far. He needed to do this if for no other reason than to decide what else he might want to find out. He felt for a minute he was living in a movie, waiting for the end to wrap all the questions up, and yet, he wasn't sure it would be that easy. The first task would be to think this through.

"Sandy, would you like to walk back to my place? You've left your car there anyway." He smiled at Sandy, thinking about all he had learned.

"Mom, you do look tired. Before we go, I want to thank you for telling me this. I know how hard it must have been for you. I also want to say that what you've told me doesn't change anything. You're my mom and always will be, just like dad." He kissed his mother goodbye and hugged her tightly. June and Sandy also embraced before the couple left.

Sandy and Ron headed out into the crisp night air, the dark cut only by the haze thrown from the streetlights. The temperature had dropped several degrees since they had arrived and Ron shivered when he reached the sidewalk, but he wasn't sure if it was the cold that caused it or not. They walked in silence for several blocks.

Suddenly Ron stopped and looked directly at Sandy, who had taken two extra steps past him before she realized he had stopped. She turned to look at him.

"Sandy, I know we've only known each other for a short time, but I feel like we're old friends. If you want to know the truth, I've felt that way since we first met. I know that sounds crazy, given the circumstances. Now all this suddenly gets thrown at me and I need to know something." He paused for several seconds, keeping his eyes locked on hers in the dim light.

"Is this more than you bargained for when we started seeing each other? All this baggage and mystery I mean?"

With everything else going through his head, Ron felt he had to know where he stood with her. That was at least something he might have some control over. Something he could hold on to during this turbulent time.

He was hoping he could at least have her remain as a stable in his life. Although he had dated women before, none had meant as much to him as Sandy did. Ron hoped she felt the same way.

Sandy looked into Ron's eyes for several seconds before answering his questions. He waited anxiously for her reply, silently praying that she would not just walk out of his life at this moment. If she did, he could understand that, but still . . .

Finally she smiled. "Yes, Ron, it's definitely more than I bargained for. Who could have expected news like that? Does it mean our friendship needs to change? No. It just makes things more interesting. And by the way, I liked you when we first met as well, even though at the time I was working on the assumption that you had somehow assaulted your aunt. So how crazy is that?" She smiled at him. The streetlights cast shadows on their faces.

"Look Ron, some things we have control over and some we don't. We can't change our past, but we can hope to make the best of our future. Let's get to your place and have a drink. It's to cold to stand here in the street and have this conversation." Sandy took his hand in hers. Ron felt the strength of her spread through him.

Silent Secrets

That answer was exactly what Ron had been hoping for. He leaned into her and kissed her gently on the mouth, right there on the street. When they parted, Sandy and Ron walked quickly the remainder of the way, hand in hand, without a word between them. None were needed.

They welcomed the warmth when they entered the house. Ron made a drink for each of them, Ron and Sandy sat together on the couch in the clean, spacious living room.

"You know, you sounded like my dad out there . . ." Ron hesitated, unsure of exactly what he was trying to say.

"Hey, what's that? I remind you of your dad? What kind of thing is that to say to a lady?" Sandy asked jokingly, punching Ron on the arm as she asked.

By her tone, Ron could tell she was trying to lighten the mood. He appreciated her sense of humour and her willingness to stick around. He leaned toward her, kissing her lightly on the lips. She kissed him back and everything suddenly else did not matter. Their bodies, warmed by the heat of the house as well as the drinks, melded together like a soft leather glove. Time slowed, yet raced like lightning.

Nature has the wonderful ability of putting life in perspective. For the first time in his life, Ron spent the night in his aunt's bedroom. Because he was not alone, the feel of the room was forever changed. The past was swept from the room and replaced by a positive memory forever. The night lasted forever.

In the morning, Sandy made hot, fresh coffee while Ron created fluffy cheese omelets and toast for breakfast. He and Sandy enjoyed this meal in the bright, sun filled, and casual atmosphere of the kitchen. They smiled often at each other, occasionally reaching out to touch hands. Sandy finally, reluctantly, said she had to get ready for work and reality intruded on the perfect domestic scene. Ron decided he could get used to this, a life of omelets and work schedules with this woman who accepted him for what he was, even though right now he wasn't sure he knew what that was. Monday was just around the corner. Ron had papers to mark and weekly plans to write out for the classroom. Yes, this could work, he decided.

Sandy agreed to return after her shift and they would eat a late dinner. In the mean time, Ron could complete his own work. Half way through the day, while reading an essay assignment he was struggling to mark, it occurred to Ron that perhaps his aunt had made some mention of the events of years ago in her many notebooks. She wrote everything else down, why not something as important at that?

The remainder of the essays lay unmarked on the dining room table while Ron surrounded himself with book upon book on the living room floor. By the time Sandy arrived several hours later, he had looked through most of the books that had been in the living room. They contained little more than day-to-day events, the canning of the produce, Ron's visits, the occasional complaint about the neighbourhood, lists of what she needed from the store. Boring notations for the most part. Nothing at all that related to her early-married life or her two children. Ron's eyes swam from the strain.

Sandy stood smiling at him in the doorway while Ron explained what he was doing. She agreed it had been a good idea, but also pointed out that it was unlikely the events of so long ago would be in books this new. Ron winced at the thought, feeling stupid that he had missed something so obvious. His mind was clearly on over load. Regardless, Sandy was back.

While preparing their supper of salmon in dill sauce with mushrooms and wild rice, which was a new and tantalizing meal for Ron, they discussed the possibility of Edith having documented her early life.

"Maybe you're right, Ron. Edith may have written down something about her husband."

"Yeah, but where do I start." Ron asked.

"Look, my police training says she likely did. Being a woman, especially one that was as much in love as your mother said . . . Well, it makes sense that she would have written something. We just have to find it." Sandy squeezed his hand and smiled.

"What could have happened, is what I want to know" Ron said, stirring the dish before him.

"Well, the way I figure it, two things could have happened" Sandy volunteered. "The first possibility was that Joseph had discovered something that concerned him about the bond between Edith and Emily. What ever this was had made him leave, without notice to any one, in order to protect his daughter." Ron just looked at her, considering this idea.

"Okay, what's your other idea"? he asked.

"Something happened that caused Joseph and Emily to disappear, but not by choice, without a trace. What ever that was," Sandy surmised, "it was traumatic enough to make Edith not report this or try to find them over the years."

Ron surmised that given the gun they had found and no explanation about the disappearance to Edith's family, this seemed the more likely possibility.

While supper simmered and the couple had a drink on the back porch in the cool air, they discussed the merits of each possibility.

"Okay, let's look at the first possibility." Sandy stated. "Joseph just decided to leave with Emily. Why would he do that? What could he have found out that would force him to choose between his children? From what your mom said, he was very happy with his life. He and Edith were happy together with the life and family they had created. Something very major would have had to happen to make him just pick up and leave."

Ron had to agree that it didn't make sense just to pick up and leave, not if what his mother had said was true. He let Sandy continue on her train of thought while he processed the possibilities.

"Not only that, why leave with one child and not the other? It's not like he wouldn't know where to find you on that day. You were with his sister in law and clearly they had a good relationship. I can't really buy into that one. It doesn't make much sense with what we know so far. I'm assuming, of course, that your mom was right about Edith and Joseph's relationship. There are things that happen behind closed doors that no one else knows about, but your mom seems very clear that this was a good marriage. We have nothing to prove other wise." She paused for a sip of her drink. Ron was nodding his head in agreement. She made a good argument.

"So, on the other hand, what if something happened to Joseph and Emily? Something that prevented them from being here, like an accident or something?" Sandy let the thought hang in the air, pulling her sweater tighter against the chilly air.

"Again, I'm not sure this makes total sense. If Edith knew what had happened to them, it would seem like she would try to get her husband and daughter back if possible, or at least tell her only sister about it."

"I know, I can't figure out why she wouldn't tell mom." Ron said, putting his arm around Sandy to ward off the damp air.

"And for that matter, why not keep you here with her, her only son? Why was she so insistent that you stay with her sister?" Sandy reached up to hold the hand which lay gently on her shoulder.

"Maybe I did something? Is that possible, that I did something but don't remember anything about it?" Ron suddenly asked, the thought scaring him.

"Well, I guess anything is possible, but that doesn't seem likely. She kept a very close eye on your growing up. Very protective.

It seems to me that, logically thinking, she must have been afraid of something. Right now I just can't figure out what. Worse case scenario, if she did cause their disappearance, why would she not want her only son back? What could have happened that would make her do something like that? Thinking about the whipping, it seems she was trying to atone for something, but was it something she did or something she couldn't prevent? That's the big question to be answered, I think. Also, I keep going back to her eccentric behaviour. That and the things we've found so far, the gun and the toys downstairs."

Hearing Sandy outline everything like this just caused Ron to be more confused. Would the answers ever be revealed, he wondered.

The couple paused in their conversation to watch a flock of Canada Geese fly overhead, squawking as they flew, a sure sign winter was very near. Even this flock was late in leaving, frost had already been seen several mornings. Usually Ron didn't like seeing this, the geese leaving the area for warmer climates, but right now, sitting here with Sandy, he was not bothered by the sight at all. At least, he thought, it was something he understood and could both predict and expect.

Ron finally broke the silence. "What I don't understand is. If she didn't want me as a child, why insist that I visit all the time. You know, the more I learn about her, the more questions I have. I think I'm going to keep reading those notebooks anyway. She must have kept them for a reason, although she did keep a lot of other junk as well." He paused again, gathering his thoughts. He knew his thoughts were scattered. Sandy sat quietly beside him, gazing at the yard, but not interrupting his train of thought. For this he was grateful. Sometimes a sounding board that you trusted made all the difference.

"All kinds of things seem strange to me." Ron continued, more to himself than any one. "She grew this entire garden, but gave it all away. Why would anyone do that?"

Ron gestured towards the large yard. Right now it was empty of any produce, yet throughout his memory, it had always been filled with such wonderfully tended vegetables. Ron sat quiet for several more minutes. Sandy let him process his thoughts. She recognized his need to come to terms with all this on his own.

"She gave everything away, me included. She kept all the junk, but gave away the good things. At least that's how I see things. She used a whip on her own back. She kept an old gun; loaded I might add, frozen in her freezer. She died battered and malnourished, surrounded by food . . ." Ron trailed off, not able to articulate everything that was puzzling him.

Sandy reached for his hand, trying to give him some sense of stability. "The way I see all this, it seems to me that she must have felt she needed to protect you, not send you away because she didn't want you. She made sure you had a good life, which based on everything you've told me, you did. She kept a very close eye on you as you grew up. When people do that, they usually are trying to protect someone, not hurt them. What we have to determine is this; was she protecting you from herself or from someone else"? Sandy left the question open ended, hoping Ron would be able to think though both possibilities.

Looking at the situation this way, hearing Sandy put this spin on the information, made Ron feel better, but not any less confused. He was so glad he had Sandy here to keep him grounded. The strong women in his life had always been able to do this, and Ron knew full well this was true.

Over the next several days, Ron and Sandy fell into a routine of working and spending their free time together. They talked a lot about Ron's family, trying to figure out what they knew and what they didn't. Ron enjoyed this time. Sandy was a very good listener and besides, it was nice to have some one in his life again. He was sad Edith had died before Sandy could meet her. He was pretty sure Edith would have liked and appreciated Sandy and her spunky attitude.

Chapter 12

Ron had the weekend to himself because Sandy was away on ballistic training for two days. He set to work correcting papers and projects. Ron was pleased see improvements in some of his grade seven students' skills in presenting the historical information he had been trying to teach them. He made a special effort to find a positive comment for each one, knowing how important that would be for all the students in his class. Christmas break would soon be here and strangely, Ron had made no plans to relocate to a warmer climate as he usually did. The snow outside, although not very deep yet, did not bother him as much as usual. Sandy's companionship was the reason for this new attitude to the cold, Ron was sure. The warmth inside balanced this, making the winter more tolerable than ever before.

By Sunday morning, his papers finished, he decided he needed a change of pace to get his mind completely off the troubling information his mother had given him a few weeks before. He had thought about all that too much and was now only going in circles.

He decided to paint the kitchen, like he had planned to before his conversation with his mother. With this thought, he set to work buying paint and supplies. He had chosen a basic, boring but clean white. Maybe, he thought, Sandy could help him with some other renovation suggestions to bring the old style kitchen up to the more present standards of use. When she returned from her weekend course, he would ask her what she thought.

Ron had missed seeing her in the last couple days, although she had called last night and they had spoken on the phone for about an hour. He realized then that he was for sure in love, as crazy as it seemed. Life again had presented him with options and this time he was determined to reach for them.

When the walls were painted, Ron looked around the kitchen proudly. He was hoped Sandy would be impressed with the transformation made just from the new clean layer of paint. He had painted all day. In the end, the effect was dramatic. Gone were the old flowers of the stained wallpaper, making even the old linoleum on the floor look somewhat better. Ron had already decided he would put in an island; the room was certainly big enough. He was beginning to like being a homeowner, being able to make changes without consulting anyone.

As he carried all the used paint supplies to the basement, he noticed the area where the old shelf had been. He had not been back to the basement since being summoned to his mothers' home for supper.

He could see light coming through some of the old boards, along with a cold draft. He decided this problem also needed to be fixed or he would end up with drafts like he had in his old apartment, which he definitely didn't want to have. That life was in his past. As he had been told so many times over the last few weeks, he needed to live in the now and look to the future, not dwell on the past.

Even though it was already getting late, Ron decided to take out the boards barely covering the hole and find out what supplies he might need to fix the problem. This would keep him busy until Sandy arrived later this evening, as she had promised to do during their long conversation last night. She had promised to come over and see him when she returned to town. He would show her what he had accomplished and they could enjoy the rest of the evening together, possibly even the entire night.

As he pulled the top boards off, he could see that the hole behind the boards had once been a window. He could just see outside with the faint light casting shadows over the yard behind the house. The glass on the outside was dirty and cracked, but still mostly intact. Funny, Ron thought, I've never noticed a window outside.

It appeared to be a window opening having been covered by wood from the inside, though it wasn't a perfect fit. Ron decided maybe his dad had come over to fix this for Edith, one of the many tasks he had performed here for her over the years. Or maybe Joseph had done this before his mysterious disappearance, he thought grimly. Edith probably thought it was just easier to block it up than fix it; also, it would prevent intruders.

A window here would certainly be a good idea, he thought, it would let light into the otherwise windowless space. A new window would not be hard to put in and he was sure he could do this tomorrow after work. The final boards came grudgingly free, but what they revealed sent Ron into another tailspin.

He stood still, looking at the contents of this small hidden space between the boards and the glass, not knowing what he saw and yet knowing full well. He saw the rose bush branches on the outside while trying to focus on what else was there. The wind brushed the branches of the rose bushes against the glass.

He tentatively reached out, but pulled his hand back at the last minute, unsure what he wanted to do.

Finally he sat on the cold concrete floor amid the boards he had removed, looking at the newly exposed space. His head was spinning, and his eyes were reeling in and out of focus. The cold air came in now through the poorly fitted glass, but Ron no longer cared. So much made sense to him now, he thought, and yet again, nothing did; more pieces of the puzzle making the puzzle bigger and bigger with every possibility. He wanted Sandy.

Ron had no idea how long he sat frozen there until he heard Sandy calling his name from above.

"I'm in the basement," was all he could manage in a strangled voice.

He heard but didn't really process the sound of Sandy coming down the steps. She called his name when she reached the bottom, causing him to jump guiltily, although he did not know why.

"Ron, what's going on, why are you sitting down here?" She was looking only at Ron, the concern evident in her voice. She had not yet noticed the window. All Ron could do was look at her, then point at the opening. Sandy turned to look, a puzzled look coming over her face.

"What is that, Ron?"

"I don't know what it is for sure, but I know what I think it is. It looks like a coffin for a very small child, doesn't it? For some reason, that's what I thought when I first found it. Sandy, I need help here." Ron looked at her pleadingly, hoping she would offer some help. He had no idea what to do at this point.

"Okay, let me take a closer look. Grab that flash light over there and give me some more light." Sandy moved toward the window. Her directions began to break the spell of helplessness Ron had been under. He grabbed the flashlight and shone the beam on the object contained in the space.

"Alright. Let's look at this logically. What I see is a wooden box, crudely made but well preserved. It's been here awhile judging from the cobwebs and dust. Look, there's a book sitting underneath as well. Let's take a look at that first. I don't want to disturb the box too much yet. Do you have a camera? We should take a picture of this before we take out the book. Maybe we're totally wrong about this, but in case we're not, the investigator is going to want to see exactly what was first found." Her police training kicked in required or not. He passed her the flashlight and followed her directions.

Ron went upstairs to get the camera while Sandy remained in the basement, assessing the items and thinking on the possible meaning of the scene. Sandy thought she knew exactly what Ron had stumbled onto in the dank basement. She wished she had arrived earlier, been there when Ron first found this area. She glanced up the stairs, hearing his movements in the kitchen. Her heart ached for him and the turmoil he was feeling.

Ron returned slowly with the camera, which he placed in her outstretched hand. He could do nothing more than stand there, looking at the gaping hole.

After taking several pictures of the scene as it presented itself, Sandy reached out and took the book from beneath the box. Dust floated all around as she did so. Thankfully, it did not appear to have gotten very wet, at least on the outside.

Together she and Ron sat on the floor and opened the small notebook to the first page. Ron turned his head away when he saw the writing and asked Sandy to read it to him. He couldn't bring himself to read the words himself; afraid and excited at the same time of what the book would say.

"You read it, Sandy" he implored in a strangled voice.

He had seen the familiar looping letters on the page, leaving no question as to the books author. Sandy skimmed the page, and then began reading aloud the faded words from the long hidden book.

"'I will forever have to live with what happened here. I will forever regret not being brave enough to do what I should have done so many years ago, the price being my family, my life. A price I can never repay. I can only hope that my son Ronny grows up to be as wonderful a man as his father Joseph was. For Emily, I hope she is at peace. For Joseph, I will be forever grateful.'"

Sandy stopped reading and turned to Ron, who remained staring at the box while listening to the words. Slowly he closed his eyes, his head dropping toward his chest. His face was devoid of any readable emotion.

"Ron, before we go any further, I think I should call the station and have them send someone over. We both know where this is going, I think." Sandy said gently, laying her hand on his shoulder.

"She killed them, didn't she?" was all he could say. Sandy remained silent, knowing Ron needed to process this for himself.

"Why?" he muttered, almost to himself. "If I had been here that day, would she have killed me too?" Ron couldn't take his eyes from the window ledge and the small box he knew had contained his sister for over 30 years.

Sandy reached out to him and helped him to his feet. "Let's go up stairs and I'll make the call. We can finish reading this while we wait. There's nothing else for us to do down here."

Ron shuffled up the stairs, his legs working on automatic, his brain no longer able to fully respond to his body's commands. He fell onto the couch as Sandy made the call beside him. He could hear her voice but what she was saying didn't register. When she finished, she sat beside him on the couch and took his hand in hers.

"Ron, I know how hard this must be for you. At least now we know where your sister is. If what we're thinking is right, something must have happened to make Edith do what she did. Let me read the rest of this notebook and maybe we can figure out what that was. One way or the other, this should give us some answers." Sandy said quietly. Ron nodded his head silently.

By the time the detectives and squad cars had arrived, Ron and Sandy had most of the answers to the many questions the discovery had brought, along with most of the other questions that had been floating around over the last few months. Ron sat quietly while the police worked below him to remove the box from the basement. When they had opened it and discovered the tiny remains inside, the coroner had been called in, not that it was necessary; there was no question that the child inside was dead.

Little remained even of the clothing she had worn, beyond some fragments of lace from her dress and bonnet. The small skeleton barely filled the box. A small crucifix hung around her neck. When the detective showed this to Ron, he recognized it as being similar to one he himself owned, long packed away some where with the remains of his own childhood. The irony of this was not lost on him.

Sandy did most of the talking to the police, all friends of hers from the department. She knew their language and what information they needed to know up front. When she had finished explaining the situation to them, they set to work, leaving Ron just to watch, an outsider in his own life.

When the box, along with its contents, had been removed and the book read through, Sandy told Ron the police had agreed to return in the morning. They would require a backhoe to finish the job the discovery had started. There was no urgency in the details. Ron could only nod.

Even before the house was clear of these strangers, Ron had fallen asleep on the couch, exhausted by the events of the evening and over load of information. His mind could process no more for tonight. His last thought before falling asleep was . . . 'I wonder if Sandy likes the kitchen?'

He awoke in the morning with a sore neck and a pounding headache. Sandy was still asleep, curled up in the chair beside him, still fully dressed as he was. Ron stood, trying to work the kink out of his neck while he walked stiffly to the kitchen. He put on a pot of coffee. A full pot. He was going to need it. Looking around the newly painted kitchen, Ron couldn't help but think that the new kitchen was the reason for all that he had found last night. He couldn't decide if he'd ever paint again.

Sandy came up behind him, giving him a hug, startling him with her quietness. They both laughed. It sounded good in the house.

Over a cup of the freshly brewed coffee, they agreed to call his mother and have her come over early this morning. She deserved to finally know what had happened so long ago. They would tell her what they now knew, hopefully before the work men arrived. This was not the kind of news she needed to read in the paper or hear on the radio. Ron also contacted work, begging off yet another day. He realized he had never missed this many days of work ever before.

June had been somewhat surprised to be called out of her home so early on a Monday morning and yet she was intrigued after speaking to Sandy enough to agree to come. As they waited for her to arrive, Ron and Sandy discussed what all this meant, for Ron and for June. Both agreed it was best to tell June everything about the contents of the book and the small coffin. Ron shuddered at the word, but a coffin was exactly what he had found.

The police had agreed to wait until the afternoon before calling in the workman and even then, it might be that they could not come until the following day. The police would thankfully take care of that task.

Ron thought this arrangement was best. That way he and Sandy would have a chance to explain to his mother without the interruption of backhoes and workman in the yard. He was very grateful Sandy had agreed to help him with this unwelcome task. He could not imagine what he would do without her.

Ron greeted his mother at the door, hugging her tight as she entered.

"Ron, what's wrong? You're as white as aa sheet. Are you sick?" June instinctively reached up to touch his forehead as they separated at the door.

Even after talking everything out with Sandy, he didn't know how to tell her what they had discovered about her sister and the others. He could not yet think of them as his father and sister, let alone his grand father. He decided it would be best to start with the discovery of the boarded up window, and let the rest evolve from there.

"I'm not sick, mom. Come on in. We need to talk." He lead her through to the kitchen.

June sat at the table, listening carefully to Ron's quiet voice, but glancing often between him and Sandy, trying to guess what they had to say. From their sullen faces she knew that something bad had happened. June waited patiently.

When Ron told her about the boarded up window in the basement, she told him she already knew that. She said she had mentioned it to Edith many years ago when she had noticed from the basement that it had been boarded up. Edith had told her the glass had broken and she couldn't afford to get it fixed. After that, the yard in front of the window had slowly been filled with the beautiful roses she grew and June had not thought of it since. Why, she asked, did Ron think she needed to know this now?

"Well mom, there's a bit more to this than just a broken window. Inside the window well, I found a small box sitting between the outside and inside ledges, behind the boards that had been nailed up. We also found a little notebook there. I'm not sure how to tell you this, but, well, inside the box was the body of a small child. A girl I would guess by the clothing that was still intact. There will be an autopsy of course, but I don't think that is really necessary. The notebook that was there made it pretty clear just who that child was; Edith's daughter, Emily."

Ron stopped talking and watched his mother. She sat very still, her hands folded on the table in front of her as he had seen her do so many times over the years. June looked from Ron to Sandy, not believing what she was hearing; yet knowing they were not lying about such a horrible thing. Tears formed at the corners of her eyes. Her brow furrowed as she tried to understand the news. The emotional impact of the tragic news was evident on her face as she sat quietly. Ron knew exactly how she felt.

Finally she said, very quietly, "I always wondered, you know, could Edith have hurt that baby, could she have somehow lost her mind and done something like this? That certainly explains why Joseph left her. But why didn't he come to get you from my house? That man loved both his children with all his heart . . ." June wondered aloud as she looked at both Ron and Sandy.

"Mom, Edith didn't kill Emily. How can I say this?" Ron paused and glanced at Sandy for support.

"Mom, it was your father who killed Emily. He also killed Joseph at the same time. That's why Joseph never came for me. They all died the same day, right here in this house." Ron said gently. He was still unable to think of Joseph as his father, regardless of having been told this already.

"My father? What are you talking about? Edith and I never saw that man after the night we fled the cabin. I didn't even know if he was even still alive. He killed Emily and Joseph? How? Why?" June's eyes were big; the colour had drained from her face. She looked scared, but of what, Ron was not sure.

"Some of the pages from the book are ruined, but from what we could make out, Edith wrote every thing down in that one book and hid it for safe keeping, I guess. Along with her baby girl." Sandy said gently.

"It seems that while Joseph and Emily were gone out to the store, and you had me at the beach on that day, your father arrived here. Edith doesn't really say how he came to find her or maybe she never knew." Ron tried to recall everything they had read.

"She says he surprised her right here in the kitchen and demanded to know where you were. It sounds like he wanted his little girl back, even though you would have been a grown woman by that time. When Edith didn't tell him, he started looking around the house, dragging her with him. She says he was drunk, so he was likely as mean as he had been when you were young." Ron paused, letting his mother take everything in. June remained quiet, needing to hear the entire story.

"For some reason," Ron continued, "he decided she owed him money for taking you away from him all those years before. He had a gun and forced her upstairs to where she and Joseph kept a small amount of emergency cash in their bedroom. Edith probably just wanted to get him out of the house before Emily and Joseph returned, or maybe even me. From what we read in her notes, as they reached the top of the stairs, Joseph did return home and surprised them both. When he saw what was happening, he ran up the stairs to try to save his wife." At this, June nodded. She could she Joseph doing that as if it were happening before his eyes. He would protect Edith with his life.

"Your father shot him as he neared the top. He still had Emily in his arms." Ron paused in his telling to catch his breath.

"Joseph's fall down the steps caused him to land on Emily, killing her in the fall. From what's in the book, it looks like Edith then reacted by pushing Jack down the stairs, probably trying to get to Joseph and Emily. When Jack landed close to the bottom, his neck must have been broken. Edith wrote about having to get him down the last few steps. The book also says that all three bodies are here at the house. Jack and Joseph are buried out in the garden."

Ron stopped talking and held his mother's hand. The book had contained other information, but for now, Ron felt he had provided most of the important parts.

June said nothing, just continued to stare. Finally she looked from Ron to Sandy several times. The tears that had sat in the corner of her eyes suddenly tumbled down her cheek. Sandy passed her a tissue, which she took gratefully.

"I can't believe this; that poor woman. Why didn't she go to the police, why not tell Austin and I?" She shook her head in disbelief. Ron and sandy remained quiet, experience telling them she needed to ask these questions.

"Why didn't she ever tell me about this?" June repeated, almost to herself. Her voice cracked as she dabbed at the tears. Ron and Sandy both knew how she felt. He gave her a few more minutes before continuing.

"From the comments in the book, it looked like she was afraid she would be charged with killing Jack and even possibly charged with setting your old home on fire all those years ago. Your father must have escaped before the fire took full hold, but it certainly looks like she did try to kill him when you two left." Sandy explained.

"I don't really understand everything yet, but my guess is that Edith felt guilty about trying to kill her father or maybe even guilty about not succeeding. She had managed to protect you by getting you away from him all those years ago, only to have him return years later and destroy her own family. I would imagine she buried them here and told every one he had run off to protect both her and you. June, she wanted you to raise her son to be sure Ron wouldn't be hurt if she was found out. Strangely, given the circumstances, I understand her logic on one level. She thought she was protecting the only family she had left. I'm sure over time we'll figure out the rest, but a lot of things are certainly more clear now." Ron was watching his mother closely as Sandy spoke.

June nodded her head. "So she wanted to be sure Ron was okay, she hid her fear all these years and secretly punished herself every day. My god, if only I had known. She was only trying to protect her family, protect me; she didn't really murder anyone. No one would have blamed her for what happened, would they? If only she had understood that, things could have been so different. What's going to happen now, Sandy? Can she be charged with anything now? Will Ron or I be charged with anything?" June looked worried as this thought occurred to her.

"There is no one to charge with anything, June. The coroner will do autopsies on the three bodies once the men have been found in the yard. I'm pretty sure they'll find just what Edith said would be there and that they will have died just as she described." Sandy told her confidently.

"Her notes say she buried Jack under the vegetable garden and Joseph under the rose bushes. How she managed to get them out there is anyone's guess, but likely she dug up the areas first and moved them at night so as not to be seen. That would explain why you couldn't contact her for several days. She likely hid the gun in the freezer, afraid that somehow everything would be found out if the gun was found." Sandy held June's hand, glancing at Ron as she did.

"I know this is really hard for you, the both of you, but I think Edith suffered her whole life for what happened that day and I doubt any one could have helped her deal with this any better than she did herself." Sandy tried to console.

June stood and reached for her coat. "Ron, call me a cab will you? I really need to go home. I can't stay here right now."

"Are you sure, mom? Do you want me to come back with you?" Ron asked. He was worried about her. As hard as this discovery had been on him, he at least had Sandy to help him. His mother had no one.

"No, Ron, you stay here and see this through. It's time for an end to all this. I don't want to be here when they start looking for those bodies. I'll call you later this evening. You call me if you need anything before then. Sandy, will you please stay and help him with this?" June pleaded with Sandy. Sandy nodded her head in agreement and let mother and son say their goodbyes in private.

When Ron returned from seeing his mother off, Sandy was sitting at the table, a fresh cup of coffee in her hands.

"You know, Ron, as strange as this all is, some of the things Edith did make a lot more sense the more I think about them. She felt guilty for a number of things and flogged herself for years because of it. She grew all that food to cover up the body of her father but couldn't bring herself to eat it. She also couldn't see it all go to waste because of how she had grown up, so she gave it all away. She tended those roses with love and care, wanting to make sure Joe's resting place was beautiful and well cared for, yet never exposed. I would imagine she couldn't bring herself to bury her baby girl outside in the cold and rain, so she made a crypt in the basement, but at the same time, she left an explanation in case everything was somehow discovered. I'm sure that's why she left you this house; she knew you would eventually find out everything. Maybe she was looking for forgiveness from you as well. The flogging in front of the family picture, I'm no psychiatrist, but I would guess she was blaming herself for their deaths, even though you and I know it was not her fault."

"She didn't need my forgiveness." Ron said. "Now, with everything I know, I understand she made sure I was well cared for and loved. She gave me a life any child would envy. For that I will be forever grateful. I'm just sorry she had to suffer by herself for so long." Ron said sadly.

"Look Ron, why don't we go to my place? I'll call the station and let them know where we'll be if they want us to return. A change of scenery is probably a good idea right now. I'll even make you lunch if you're nice to me." she joked, sliding her hand into his.

As they left the house to go to her car parked down the block, Mr. Wells came down his steps to speak to the couple.

"Ronny, are you all right? Mrs. Wells was so worried last night when she saw the police arrive. You haven't been hurt, have you? Did some one break in or something?" Mr. Wells asked the couple.

Ron looked quickly at Sandy, then back to Mr. Wells.

"You tell Mrs. Wells that I am just fine, Mr. Wells. There's going to be a bit of activity in the back yard today or tomorrow; I hope the noise doesn't bother her too much. Please give her my apologies, if it does. Also, please tell Mrs. Wells that I thank her for being such a good friend to Edith all these years, I think it meant a lot to her."

"Well now, I'll do that son. I know she'll be pleased to hear that. Are you making some changes to the back yard?"

"I think I'll be making a lot of changes over the next little while, Mr. Wells, starting with taking my girl here to have lunch. Other than that, I'm just having a few things removed from the yard. I don't think Edith would have minded. Bye for now, we'll be back to see you later." Ron shook hands with Mr. Wells.

Ron took Sandy's hand as they continued down the street, the trees now free of the beautiful autumn leaves. Fall had brought the beginning of a time when life had changed so suddenly for him. Looking at the frosty trees now, Ron thought all that was right, a little change for every one and a new start all the way around was in order.

Ron planned to start with lunch with Sandy while the changes in the yard took place.

The rest could wait for another day.

Edwards Brothers Malloy
Oxnard, CA USA
July 25, 2013